THE FORT█████S

THE **FORTUNES** OF **TEXAS**

MILITARY MAN

———— ⚓ ————

USA TODAY BESTSELLING AUTHOR

Marie Ferrarella

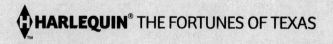

HARLEQUIN® THE FORTUNES OF TEXAS

Recycling programs
for this product may
not exist in your area.

ISBN-13: 978-1-335-68080-8

Military Man

First published in 2005. This edition published in 2019.

Copyright © 2005 by Harlequin Books S.A.

Printed in U.S.A.

™ www.Harlequin.com

To Patience Smith and the team we have become.

Chapter 1

"You know I wouldn't ordinarily be asking you to do this, but..."

Lt. Collin Jamison heard his cousin's voice awkwardly trail off on the other end of the line. Collin's lips curved slightly in an understanding smile. That had always been his gift, for as far back as he could remember. Understanding. Although it took no special gift to know where Emmett was coming from.

His cousin had trouble asking people for favors, even from someone he'd once been close to, the way they once had been.

Granted it was a hell of a favor to ask. But at least, since he'd sought him out like this, it meant that Emmett had decided to come back to join the living. That alone would have had Collin saying yes, no matter what the obstacles.

It wasn't easy for Collin to arrange free time. When you worked as an Army Ranger for CIA Special Operations, specializing in manhunts and intelligence gathering, it wasn't exactly as if you were just another easily replaceable cog.

But he had a lot of time coming to him, time he'd never bothered using because there hadn't been anything else he'd rather be doing than his job.

Things could be managed, Collin thought. Things could *always* be managed.

Collin shifted the receiver to his other ear. He'd barely walked into the small, two-bedroom condo he owned right outside of Langley, Virginia, when the phone had rung, demanding his attention. He'd thought it was a call to come in for a new assignment.

In a way, he supposed it was.

Exchanging quick, perfunctory pleasantries for less than two minutes, Emmett had swiftly filled him in as to why he'd called. Even when they were young, Emmett had never believed in wasting time. Neither did he. That was why they got along so well.

"Yeah, I know," Collin said in response to his cousin's awkward pause. "I've got to admit, it's a hell of a surprise, hearing from you. Uncle Blake said that you had gone off somewhere into the mountains in New Mexico to be by yourself." He recalled the conversation in its entirety. Blake Jamison had been sincerely worried about his youngest son, not knowing if Emmett was going to permanently withdraw from life, or if he just needed time to come to terms with the things he'd witnessed during the course of his work as an FBI special agent.

"I did."

He heard Emmett sigh quietly on the other end, as if a part of him still wanted to be back there, hidden in the mountains, away from the world. Collin knew how that could be. There were times when he'd thought seriously about just saying the hell with everything and retreating himself. That usually lasted until the next interesting case came along to challenge him. He was no good with free time. Free time made you think.

"I needed some peace and quiet," Emmett

was saying. As always, his cousin was given to understatement.

For a while there Collin had worried about Emmett's sanity. Everyone thought about running away, but very few ever did it. Those who did generally invited speculation about the state of their mental health.

But now that Emmett was back, Collin breathed a little easier. "Couldn't find any, huh?" he joked.

His uncle Blake had told Collin that when Emmett's older brother, Christopher, had turned up murdered, it just intensified Emmett's desire to stay away from the world. It was only after his father had made the pilgrimage to his shack to tell him that Christopher had been killed by Jason, the brother both he and Christopher had watched descend into madness, that Emmett had snapped out of his depression and left his self-imposed exile to battle the "bad guys" again. This time, the bad guy was his older brother.

"No, it's not that," Emmett responded wearily to his cousin's joke. "The world just won't let me alone." He took a deep breath and reiterated his initial plea. "I need your help in finding Jason."

Collin didn't bother saying the obvious, that

Emmett had greater resources than him to employ. Or the more obvious, that the FBI was never thrilled having someone from the CIA nosing around. He said, instead, what they both knew to be true.

"Jason's sick, Emmett. He has been for a long time now." Jason had been different as a boy, given to hero-worshiping their grandfather to the point that it became a near obsession. All of Farley Jamison's past history became Jason's by proxy, to cherish and, more importantly, to vindicate.

"No," Emmett contradicted, his voice harsh. "He's evil. You know that."

Yes, Collin thought, he supposed he did. Accustomed as he was to the ugly underbelly of the world, he still found it hard to pin that label on someone whose blood ran through his own veins.

Pausing, Collin tried to guess at Emmett's reasons for what he was doing. The brothers had never been particularly close, even as children.

"You afraid the FBI'll kill Jason if they find him?"

Emmett's voice was steely as he replied, "No, I'm afraid he'll wind up killing someone else. He's my flesh and blood and I don't want that on my conscience."

Emmett always had enough conscience for three people, Collin thought. For a man who was only thirty-one, he acted as if he'd been born old. "You're not your brother's keeper, Emmett."

There was another long pause on the other end of the line. Collin wondered if he'd insulted Emmett. After all, he hadn't seen or spoken to him for a while now and people had a habit of changing.

Everyone but him, he mused.

"Maybe not," Emmett finally said, "but I'm an FBI agent. What I'm supposed to do is keep the public safe from maniacs like Jason. Frankly, I'm afraid that he'll surface somewhere and kill Ryan Fortune before I get a chance to take him down."

Collin was vaguely familiar with Fortune, mainly from newspaper articles. The billionaire rancher was the epitome of generosity, giving to so many charities that the public had lost count. Collin was also aware that there was some sort of a family connection, but he had his own world, his own concerns. The Fortunes were a world apart from him.

"Ryan Fortune? Why?"

In the background, he thought he heard someone call out, "Room Service." Emmett responded with a crisp, "Later," before continuing and telling him what he'd pieced together. "Because Grandpa's stories turned Jason's mind to the state of an overripe, rotting apple. Because Grandpa blamed the Fortunes for turning him into a pauper and making him live out the rest of his life in that state. Grandpa needed a scapegoat for his problems and an audience to hear about it. Jason adored him and now he thinks he's bringing some kind of divine justice into play.

"I know him, Collin. Jason's crazy enough and evil enough to try something desperate. I mean, if he killed Christopher because for some reason Christopher got in the way of his big 'plans,' then—"

Collin was quick to stop him. He needed confirmation. "Is that what happened?"

A rare fondness slipped into Emmett's voice. "You know Christopher. He's always—" Emmett stopped; Collin could almost feel the other man's physical pain as he corrected himself "—*was* always bent on bringing out the best in everyone. He knew Jason was obsessed with avenging Grandpa and followed him down here to Red Rock to talk him out of whatever it was he was planning." All feeling drained out of his voice. "But nobody messes with Jason. At least, that's what Jason believes."

Even as a small boy, Collin remembered, Jason had always been headstrong, always needed to be center stage, or else he was given to destroying the stage.

"So he killed Christopher." Even though Jason had been arrested and charged with the crime, with most people believing he was guilty, it was still something that Collin found difficult to say.

"And that girl who was posing as his wife," Emmett interjected. "And that guard who was transporting him to another prison."

And who knew how many others who hadn't come to light, Collin couldn't help thinking.

"Human life means nothing to him," Emmett said with utter disgust. "And a second transport guard is just barely hanging on."

"Maybe he can tell you something—" Collin began.

Emmett cut him off. Not because he felt angry or impatient, Collin knew, but because it was the way he was. Clipped and to the point.

Collin knew that was his cousin's way of keeping everything at bay except for the facts.

Emmett was not about to allow his emotions to suck him down to the depths he'd already been pulled to once.

He couldn't survive a second trip down that far.

"The guard's in a coma."

"Oh." That rather curtailed his ability to talk to the man, Collin thought. "So what exactly do you want from me?"

"I need you to do what you do best," Emmett told him. "You can get into the mind of a criminal, find him, second guess his next move."

The words were flattering, but not without foundation. Still, he did that with strangers, getting into their heads, under their skins. But in this case Emmett had an advantage over him. "He's your brother, shouldn't you be the one who's able to—"

Again Emmett cut him short. "Jason's been a mystery to me from day one. Christopher was the brother I always admired, not Jason." Collin could hear the pain in his cousin's voice. "Jason was always evil, always out for just Jason."

With one notable exception, Collin thought. "Except in the way he felt about your grandfather."

"I think he saw Grandpa as an extension of himself." Emmett made his final entreaty. "This is family business, Collin. I need someone on my side."

It was clear to Collin that even though his cousin was part of the FBI himself, the organization saw them as intruders in this case.

The request was something new for Emmett. Collin knew that his cousin was accustomed to working alone. So much so that the Bureau did not view him as a team player. But Emmett was very good at what he did, which made him a valuable asset to the FBI. Valuable assets were allowed some leeway. So when Emmett had put in for an extended leave of absence, saying he'd needed time to pull himself together, Collin knew the objections had been few. The Bureau did not want to risk having a stressed-out agent amid their number.

For a while there Collin had thought that his cousin's withdrawal from the world was destined to be a permanent one. And maybe it would have become that eventually, if family honor and Emmett's own sense of pride hadn't joined together to pull him out of the tailspin he'd found himself in.

Leaning back, Collin put his feet on his coffee table and formed the only conclusion he could from Emmett's tone. "I take it our end of the investigation is going to be unofficial."

Even if it hadn't been his choice, it would have had to be this way. "You know the Bureau frowns on their operatives handling anything that remotely involves their personal lives."

The army was the same way. He was going to have to request a leave of absence, Collin thought.

He laughed softly to himself, relishing the image. "So as far as the local law-enforcement officers are concerned, we're going to be just two pains in the butt for them."

As always, Emmett put a serious interpretation on the words. "Let me worry about the local law-enforcement officers."

Swinging his legs off the table, Collin shifted to the edge of the sofa, his attention focused on the nature of Emmett's words. "You are planning on checking in with them." He wanted to know.

Emmett was honest with him. Collin knew Emmett could never be anything less than that. "As little as possible and only when necessary. You know that every agency thinks they're supreme."

Collin grinned and laughed again, unable to help himself. "When we all know that it's only true as far as the FBI is concerned."

The easy give-and-take they'd always enjoyed as boys and then young men was still held somewhat in abeyance. Invoking the memories, he might feel comfortable around Emmett, but there was no sign that Emmett reciprocated the feeling. He seemed to be nothing but all business and as rigid as an iron bar.

"So." Emmett wanted to know. "Are you in?"

There had never been any question in Collin's mind from the moment he'd said hello and recognized Emmett's voice. "I'm in."

In what, Collin wasn't altogether sure. But at least this seemed to have drawn Emmett out of seclusion. He'd been seriously worried that his cousin had succumbed to the mind-numbing allure of alcohol to the point that there was no turning back. If trying to find Jason and bring him back to face the consequences of his actions helped dry Emmett out, then he was all for it.

And if it ultimately kept Jason from killing anyone else, that could only be a good thing.

"I'm staying at the Corner Inn in Red Rock," Emmett said. "Room twelve."

Collin was stationed in Virginia, where he now hung his hat and called home, but he could be in Texas in a matter of hours once his leave was approved. Because of the nature of his work, he was always semipacked and ready to go at a moment's notice. He never knew when the next day might find him half a world away.

"I'll be there by noon tomorrow." It was a promise he meant to keep.

"Thanks."

Hanging up, Collin rose from the sofa, prepared to return to the base he'd left less than half an hour ago. Since his case was wrapped up, getting a personal leave shouldn't be a problem, especially if he cited a family emergency. The colonel was very big on families. So much so that on the occasional times that Collin had been invited to the man's house for the purpose of socializing, Colonel Eagleton had always had an unattached female in attendance. The man fancied himself a matchmaker. Collin had once commented that his C.O. shouldn't give up his day job.

"Got another one for you, Luce," Dr. Harley Daniels announced cheerfully, coming through the rear double doors into the sterile arena where they conducted most of their work. He was pushing a gurney ahead of him. The one with the right rear squeaky wheel that defied any and all attempts to mute it.

Lucy Gatling, third-year med student, braced herself as she looked up from the small desk she occupied. She knew that the medical examiner had to be referring to yet another body upon which he was about to perform an autopsy. As a student observer, she got to watch. Right before her very first autopsy, she'd made up her mind to mentally stand apart, as if what was going on in front of her was just a movie. It helped. Some.

Lucy knew that if she was going to become a doctor worth her salt, she was going to have to get over that initial queasiness that struck every time she was faced with the prospect of looking at a dead body being dissected. There wasn't too much she could do about the queasiness, but she knew she could control her outer reaction to it.

Because she was so good at masking her emotions, no one ever had a clue as to what she was actually feeling, but that didn't negate the fact that it felt as if a tidal wave had suddenly been created within her stomach and was wrecking havoc on the coastline.

Dr. Daniels parked the gurney under the overhead lights. He was a big man, brawny and bald, more apt to be mistaken for a professional wrestler than a dedicated doctor bent on uncovering the mysteries of death.

"You know," he said, "every other student we've had here has always spent the first couple of weeks of their stay flinching every time they heard one of the gurneys approaching." He chuckled, the deep sound echoing in the Spartan-like chamber. "Hell, we had a big burly guy pass out three times before he finally requested a transfer. But you—" there was admiration in his eyes as Lucy felt them pass over her "—you're something else again."

Lucy took that as a high compliment. She'd heard that Daniels was not free with them. Her mouth curved ever so slightly.

Something else again.

That was the way her father had described her, more than once, always marveling at such stoicism in one so young.

What he hadn't known, what no one seemed to even guess at, was that her particular brand of stoicism had been put in place to keep back an ocean of tears. If she had permitted herself even the display of a single tear, Lucy knew in her heart she wouldn't be able to stop crying. Perhaps ever.

At least that was the way she'd felt for a very long time. As the only child of two parents who'd proudly served in the military, her whole life had been a series of leavings and of battling the feeling that she was being abandoned by one or the other of her parents. Sometimes both. When their tours of duty had conflicted with parenting, she'd been shipped off to her grandparents. She'd been a world traveler whose home was anywhere her suitcase went.

The nomadic lifestyle she'd been forced to lead had taught her at a very early age that she could not keep her parents at her side, nor could she remain where newly formed friendships had begun to push tender shoots through the earth and flourish. She certainly could not remain complacent or feel remotely secure because of any outer trappings.

She'd come to the realization early on that if she wanted security, she was going to have to look inward. The same was true of complacency. That only came from depending solely on herself, so that no matter where in the world she woke up or whom she found herself speaking to, she was her own person, secure and confident that she could go on despite whatever curves life suddenly threw her.

Damn but it was wearying at times to know that she was all there was.

Oh, there was her father and now that he had retired and moved close to her, that was a good thing. But strictly speaking, it almost felt as if it was too late. Lucy dearly loved Retired Lieutenant John Gatling, but she wasn't the little girl she knew he was hoping to resume a relationship with. There was no going back and picking up where they had left off. Those years had long gone. She was a woman now, had become one long before her time.

And she had become so self-reliant that no one had seen her cry when she'd been told of her mother's mysterious death halfway around the world. All she'd been told, by the military and by her father, who she suspected had no more information than she did, was that her mother had died "in the line of duty."

In the line of duty. It was a phrase that was supposed to cover a myriad of things and explain everything. It covered little and explained nothing, but she'd ceased asking for answers.

At least, answers that had to do with the military. Answers that had to do with medicine and life in general as seen through a microscope were another matter. Her naturally inquisitive mind, her desire to do good, to help, had made her turn to medicine in hopes of allowing her to act upon her good intentions. At least in the field of medicine she had a fighting chance to solve a few of the mysteries, answer a few of the questions.

Maybe, if she was very lucky, they would be the ones that counted.

Now she moved out of the doctor's way, eager to learn whatever it was that this newest victim had to silently teach her.

"What's his story?" she asked Dr. Daniels as she glanced down at the corpse. Before the medical examiner could tell her, Lucy answered her own question. "Hey, wait, isn't that one of the guards who was involved in that prisoner getaway?" She looked at the Y incision that ran the length of his torso. "Didn't you already do him?"

Looking down at the still face, she recognized the man from the front page of the newspaper. Death had taken away his color and left a pasty gray in its place, but the man's features had struck her initially because his face was almost a perfect square. Cruel though it was, that was something death hadn't altered.

"We lost the paperwork. Don't ask," Daniels said. Then his brown eyes grew serious. "We might be getting his friend down here any day now. They're keeping him alive at County, but who knows how long he's going to hang on?"

She caught an undercurrent in the physician's voice. Because of the nature of her childhood, she'd learned how to make quick assessments of the people around her. "You really like this job, don't you?"

He looked surprised that she would make the comment. After all, she was the student, he the teacher. After a moment of stony silence, his rounded cheeks widened in a smile.

"Yes, I do. Dead people don't talk back. They don't make comments about how little money you have or how inferior they think you are."

Given his size and appearance, it wasn't a stretch for her to visualize him as an adolescent who'd spent his time on the outside of the inner circle. "The right living people don't, either."

There was a warm light in his eyes as he looked at her. "You'd be surprised, Lucy. Not everyone has your keen insight."

She shrugged carelessly. Personal attention always made her uncomfortable. Unlike what she imagined the doctor had been at her age, she liked being the one on the outside. "I'm not that unique."

"I think you are."

She raised her eyes to his. For a split second their roles were reversed. "Dr. Daniels—"

He laughed, shaking his head. If he'd entertained any serious thoughts about her at a given point, Lucy knew she'd squelched them by now. "Yes, I know. You don't go out with people you work with." He paused before donning his surgical rubber gloves. "Tell me, I'm curious. How are you going to ever find yourself a husband if you keep ruling people out like that?"

Her voice was crisp. It was a question she'd answered before. "I'm not looking for a husband. I'm looking to finish my schooling and then start my career. After that's established, then I might think about a relationship."

It was a lie. She wasn't planning on ever looking into forming a lasting relationship, certainly not the romantic one Daniels was inquiring about. Romantic relationships resided in the land of uncertainty. Math and science were where all the answers were. And forensic medicine, her ultimate field of expertise, dealt in facts once they'd been uncovered.

Relationships, she had learned, both through her parents—who were not stationed in the same state, sometimes not even the same country, for months at a time—and through Jeffrey Underhill, the one boy she'd allowed herself to fall in love with at the tender age of seventeen, were far from certain or even vaguely predictable.

She liked sticking with a sure thing.

"Shall we?" Daniels asked as he slipped on his rubber gloves.

Following his example, Lucy put on her own set. It was time to find out if the guard's body contained any secrets for them.

Chapter 2

Far from being a demonstrative person, Emmett Jamison usually kept his feelings bottled up inside. Very little made him smile or show any sort of outward reaction other than a frown. At best, there were patient expressions. Even so, when he opened his hotel room door and saw Collin, his eyes seemed to light up. Without apparently stopping to think, Emmett threw his arms around him and hugged. Hard.

Surprised to say the least, Collin returned the embrace.

Taking a breath, Emmett stepped back, as if to bring himself under control. "Thanks for coming."

Collin could hear the barely bridled emotion vibrating in Emmett's voice.

"How could I not come?" They weren't just cousins, they were friends. Even when Emmett had gone off to disappear into the bottom of a bottle, from time to time he would make an effort to remain in touch. "Like you said in your phone call, you don't ask for many favors." His cousin looked wan, Collin thought, like a man coming out of a cave after a prolonged period of time, which, in a way, he supposed Emmett was. "As a matter of fact, I can't recall a single time that you ever did."

Leaning slightly to the side to see around his taller cousin, Collin peered into the room Emmett was occupying. "Still Spartan as ever, I see." He grinned. "You can take the man out of the hermit, but you can't take the hermit out of the man."

Emmett shrugged. "It's just a room. It suits my purposes."

Collin nodded. Unlike Jason, Emmett had never been one for creature comforts. He'd never required much. From the time he was old enough to purchase them himself, he owned only a sparse number of things; they never owned him.

Collin set down the single suitcase he'd

brought. "I'll just leave my things here until I get a room of my own."

He'd come to the hotel in Red Rock straight from the airport. It had taken surprisingly little effort to get here. Tentatively, when he'd gone to his C.O., he'd asked for a two-week leave of absence. Colonel Eagleton had been more than happy to grant it to him.

"I was beginning to think you didn't have a life outside of the job," his C.O. had said.

It was very nearly true. His work had become his life and vice versa. There was no time, no room, for anything else. By design.

It wasn't just that the nature of his work took him away from the place where he hung his uniform—a place very much like the one that Emmett was currently in. Collin, like his father before him, had the gift to delve into another person's mind, to take that person apart, bit by bit and to figure out what made that person act the way he did. Yet Collin had no such gift when it came to himself. Or, more to the point, to the women he interacted with.

Collin had no doubts that if one of the women he dealt with on a day-to-day basis were to show up on the other side of a Wanted poster or an assignment sheet, he would be able figure out her next move with more than some degree of certainty. However, he also knew that if that same woman were sitting at a restaurant table directly opposite him, she'd leave him clueless.

He'd long ago come to the conclusion that he had no knack for personal male-female relationships.

If he'd had, Paula would have stayed.

Hell, he thought as he watched his cousin put his suitcase inside the closet, Paula would have been his wife by now. He would have known enough to make her his wife instead of remaining engaged for six years and somehow just allowing the status quo to continue unchallenged.

But maybe there was a reason for that.

There was so much turmoil packed into his active life that when it came to the personal side of him, he craved peace. Contentment. Something to count on. He supposed wanting that made him seem dull.

And maybe he was.

The thought caused his mouth to quirk in a semi-smile. It always did. Anyone knowing the kind of life he led, a life that took him into unfriendly territory on a regular basis, always walking a tightrope and laboring beneath the constant risk of death, wouldn't have said that he had a dull bone in his body. But he did, if wanting the kind of peace and quiet he only knew secondhand made him dull. The kind of life his parents had led.

Paula would have given him that kind of life. He'd known that, felt it in his bones. But he'd allowed her to slip right through his fingers.

Not that the slippage was swift. Paula had been nothing if not patient, determined, he now realized, to wait him out. He'd certainly had a lot of time to make known his feelings about their future. The trouble was, it was always something that he'd figured would keep.

For them, he'd felt, there was always tomorrow. Except that when tomorrow finally arrived, it saw her on the arm of his best friend. Saying her vows.

He'd attended the ceremony, wished them both well with all the sincerity he could muster—and then closed up the remaining exposed portion of his heart, mentally declaring himself a failure when it came to relationships.

He didn't blame Paula. He put the blame squarely where it belonged. On his own shoulders.

And he missed Paula like hell, even years after she'd become Mrs. William Pollack.

Collin roused himself. He had no idea why thoughts of Paula, of their life together before she'd had her fill of empty dreams, was preying on his mind today. It had been a while since he'd thought about her. Not since her anniversary had gone by last month. He supposed maybe it had to do with seeing Emmett again, because Emmett belonged to those days. Days when he had been a lot younger and a lot more hopeful.

And foolish.

"So, where do we start?" he asked as he preceded Emmett into the hallway and his cousin closed and locked the hotel room door behind them, slipping the rectangular key card into his pocket. "Do we check in with the locals?"

Emmett knew that he was referring to the local police and not just the people who might have possibly witnessed something. He shook his dark head. "Not until it's absolutely necessary."

Collin understood perfectly. "Meaning, not until they stumble over us."

"Something like that." A hint of a smile crossed Emmett's lips, but then it was gone the very next moment. He led the way out into the parking lot and his car, a beat-up old

Chevy that traveled as much on faith as it did on gasoline. "I thought we might go see Ryan Fortune. I want you to meet him. I'll bring you up to speed on what I know on the way."

Collin nodded, folding his six-foot frame into the passenger side. "Sounds like the start of a plan."

The headaches were blinding now.

So much so that Ryan Fortune had been forced to finally admit to Lily that he was going to be felled by a death sentence.

His death sentence.

There'd been no getting around it. His darling Lily was far too much of a loving wife not to notice that something was horribly wrong and had been getting more so now for months. At first she'd suspected that all this secrecy had to do with another woman's designs on his affections. When he'd discovered that, he'd known it was time to tell her the truth.

So he'd sat her down, taken her hands in his and finally told her, as gently as possible, about the inoperable brain tumor that was stealing him away from his family years before he was ready to go.

They'd held each other and cried. There was nothing else to be done.

Sixty was old when you were in your twenties. But from where he was standing, it was way too young to call it a day. Or a life.

But Ryan had no power, no say in the matter. He could only make what was left of it as meaningful as was humanly possible. For himself and, far more importantly, for those he loved.

The irony of it made him smile.

He'd stand a lot better chance of succeeding in his goal if these damn headaches didn't keep insisting on interfering. Of course, if there had been no headaches, there would have been no tumor and no need to press on with such fervor to see that certain things were completed before his end. Such as his charity work.

And so he pushed on, taking life on like a contender and trying to make it all seem as if it was business as usual. Which meant not putting *anything* off until tomorrow, because tomorrow, for him, might not even exist.

It was a bitter pill to swallow. Daily.

Thinking himself past the pain, Ryan tried valiantly to concentrate on what Emmett Jamison was asking him. He'd only known the young man a short time, but was extremely impressed with Emmett, not to mention extremely grateful. It was Emmett who had put his life on the line, saving Lily from what he now knew had to have been certain death. His Lily had been kidnapped not for money, but to torment him. And the ultimate torment would have meant losing her forever. He might have done just that, if it hadn't been for Emmett. He owed the man a great deal. More than he could ever hope to repay. He wished he could do something to help Emmett find his remaining brother and bring him to justice. But there wasn't much he could do.

"I really don't know what more I can tell you, Emmett. I never knew Christopher, couldn't even help to identify his body when they dragged it from Lake Mondo."

He addressed his words to both Emmett and the cousin he'd brought with him. The latter was a tall, muscular young man of about thirty-five or so, if he was any judge. The man's weather-roughened face only added to his rugged appearance.

Ryan hadn't been surprised when Emmett told him that his cousin was a career military man. Collin looked the type. It took very little imagination to envision him sliding down a rope out of the sky like some sort of commando.

He was familiar with the bearing. The young man was quiet, polite, but there was an air of immortality about him. Navy SEALs, the Rangers, all those Special Ops people had the same air. They had to. If they began to believe in their own mortality, in their own demise, they couldn't accomplish the incredible missions they undertook or face death the way they did, with bravado and a go-to-hell attitude.

Who knew, Ryan mused, if life had turned out differently for him, maybe he would have gone into that sort of work himself.

With all his heart, he certainly wished he could tell death to go to hell at the present moment.

"I realize that, sir," Collin said politely, his voice soft, in direct contrast to the swiftness with which he could mete out punishment when called upon to do so. "But my cousin—" he nodded toward Emmett "—tells me that you had several dealings with Jason. And it's Jason we're tracking."

Collin wasn't giving away any secrets. Jason, the cold-blooded killer of his own brother and the woman who had been posing as his wife, needed to be brought back to face the justice he thought he'd eluded. Jason had

used his inherent cunning to take advantage
of whatever situation had presented itself to
him, whether it involved talking one or both
of the two men driving him to the maximum
security prison into lowering their guard, or
perhaps believing him when he offered to
bribe one or both. Collin didn't know what
had happened. No one did, because the only
three people who could provide the answers
were either dead, missing or in a coma.

So right now Collin was pinning his hopes
on Ryan Fortune, the unwitting target of Jason's unspent wrath.

"Jason," Ryan repeated, shaking his head.

Collin exchanged glances with Emmett, not
certain how to read the older man's expression. There was no fear in Ryan's voice and
no anger, both of which were emotions that he
would have expected. Instead there was sorrow, something he didn't quite grasp in this
context.

A self-deprecating smile slid along Ryan's
lips. He thought of the poor young woman,
Melissa, who'd made a rather embarrassing
and shameless play for his affections. As if
he'd ever leave his Lily after what he'd gone
through to finally marry her. Melissa's far-
from-innocent flirtation, he told himself,

should have been his first clue, his first warning that something was decidedly wrong with Jason. But even so, a man couldn't be blamed for what his wife did, and vice versa. And Ryan had always liked to believe the best of everyone. But sometimes, it appeared, a person *had* no best.

"A man hates to discover this late in the game that he is such a poor judge of character," Ryan confessed to the two strapping young men in his living room. "Jason, I'm afraid, is the perfect chameleon, being everything I thought the job needed. A go-getter from the second he walked into a room."

It had all been a ploy, a weapon Jason Jamison, who'd called himself Wilkes at the time, had used to get close to him. The intricacy of the plot overwhelmed Ryan now that he looked back at it. It was something he'd expect to find in an entertaining movie, not something he'd actually discover himself living through.

"I thought he was the perfect executive in training for my nephew's company," he continued. Ryan still found it difficult to refer to Fortune TX, Ltd. as Logan's, though his nephew had succeeded him as CEO. Ryan now acted in an advisory capacity. That was how his path had crossed Jason's. And all by Jason's design. "All the times I talked to him—and there were more than a few—I never once saw anything in his eyes to indicate that he hated me so much."

"He's a textbook sociopath, sir," Collin told him kindly. "He didn't intend for you to see. Until he's within the reach of his goal, a sociopath can be anything he needs to be. It's the nature of the beast."

Collin suppressed a sigh. This was his cousin he was talking about. Someone he'd grown up knowing. More than that, he was Emmett's brother. But one glance toward his cousin told him that Emmett felt no more kinship toward Jason than he would a rattlesnake.

Ryan cleared his throat, uncomfortable with the conversation. With his own lack of perception in the case. He looked at Emmett who had lost so much and would lose more.

Did Emmett secretly blame him, as well? Ryan would have said no, but his faith in his own abilities to read people had been badly shaken. The ache in his temples grew. "I swear I had nothing to do with your grandfather's impoverished state. I knew nothing about—"

Emmett held his hand up, curtailing any further apology. He wasn't here to erode Ryan

Fortune's pride or to foster any false sense of guilt. He wasn't his grandfather's champion, because in his estimation his grandfather and no one else was responsible for his own fate.

"Everyone knows how generous you are, Ryan," Emmett said. "News of your largesse even reaches shacks at the base of the Sandia Mountains." Emmett had never had the rapport that Jason had had with their grandfather. Maybe because he'd seen the old man for what he was. A bitter man who needed someone to blame for his lack of accomplishments, for his failures. "Grandpa's mind left him a long time ago."

"There are men who can never take responsibility for their own misfortunes," Collin commented. His mouth quirked at the unwitting use of the word. "No pun intended, sir."

Ryan nodded, forcing a smile to his lips. The pain at the back of his skull was getting worse again. He wasn't certain how much longer he could stay on his feet here, talking as if he didn't feel as though he was being beaten down to his knees.

"None taken," he told Collin, slowly meting out each word.

Noting the pained look on the older man's

face, Collin backed off. He didn't want to push or pry, not when Ryan appeared to be unwell.

"Maybe we can stop by the medical examiner's office and see if they've discovered anything that might give us a lead." Collin knew that finding out anything was going to take a great deal of finesse. Information wasn't just released to anyone, especially not in this day and age. If he flashed his credentials, it would be assumed that he was there in an official capacity, and he wasn't comfortable lying outright. But maybe, if the examiner should "accidentally" glimpse his credentials in his wallet as he went to take out something, then that would convey an official air without his having to actually state the fact.

He intended to try.

He rose from his seat and Ryan followed his lead. "You think Jason's still in the area?" the older man asked.

Collin gave him a pointed look. "You still are—and you're his prime target."

As they'd approached the house earlier, Collin had surveyed the area and had seen no security. But then, good bodyguards, the kind that Ryan needed, wouldn't have been out in plain sight. He sincerely hoped the man was smart enough to avail himself of that kind of protection.

As they walked to the living room door, Ryan turned toward Emmett. "Would you mind if I had a word with you?" Glancing at Collin, he added, "This'll only take a minute."

"Take all the time you need," Collin told him. "I'll be right outside." He indicated the hallway beyond the living room, then stepped out, giving them the privacy that was required.

Turning from the doorway, Ryan looked at the younger man with him. He saw beyond the rigid features. Emmett looked worn and yet ready to snap. A gun cocked to fire. Jason had done more damage to his own family than he'd ever done to the Fortunes he despised.

"I won't keep you…" Ryan began. As he spoke, he slipped his arm around Emmett's shoulders. "I just want you to know again how sorry I am about Christopher."

Emmett nodded, not knowing what to say. He wanted to be flippant, to say something blasé. But it wasn't in him. Not about Christopher. Christopher deserved better at his hands, even if he hadn't received it at Jason's.

"He was always the good guy in the family," Emmett remembered, a distant fondness entering his voice. "The white sheep."

Ryan thought of his own brother, gone so many years. "I know what it's like to lose a brother. They leave behind an emptiness nothing can quite fill."

Emmett's expression hardened. "Jason won't leave behind an emptiness when he's gone." He laughed shortly, a bitter taste in his mouth. "I plan to go on a three-day drinking binge to celebrate the fact that he's no longer a blot on our family name."

Ryan had no idea if that was just talk or if Emmett intended to carry out his words. He was aware of the younger man's recent self-imposed exile and the extent to which it went.

"Don't let revenge eat you up, Emmett," he warned. "That would be Jason's final triumph, turning you into a bitter man."

Emmett had become that long before Jason's path had taken him to murder their brother and that woman, as well as the guard and who knew who else. The cases he'd handled had seen to that. Lives cut down in their prime for no reason. Emmett knew that had all contributed to making him the man he was now. But Jason's actions had certainly been the proverbial icing on the cake.

And yet, in a way, they had pulled him out of the depression he'd fallen into, given his life a focus, a purpose that merely returning to work for work's sake never could have.

The irony of it made him smile as he looked at Ryan, touched by the man's concern. "Too late."

Ryan had another opinion. "We're put on this earth to help one another, Emmett."

The similarity jarred him. "You sound like Christopher."

"Then he was a wise man," Ryan told him, his smile widening despite the force of the pain assaulting his temples. "Christopher wouldn't want you to let revenge govern your life. If you let it do that, then you'll be just like Jason."

It wasn't a new thought for him. It had crossed his mind more than once. But Emmett shrugged. "Maybe we're more alike than I thought." And then, before Ryan could say anything further, Emmett added, "Don't worry. I'm an FBI agent. My job is to make sure the bad guys are separated from the good guys before they can do any harm."

Ryan remained unconvinced, although he wanted to be. "Just as long as it remains your job and you don't make it personal."

"It already is personal," Emmett said quietly. Shaking Ryan's hand, he tried to smile.

"I'll give your words a lot of thought," he promised.

"That's all I ask," Ryan replied.

Collin stopped dead.

He and Emmett had made their way into the bowels of the three-story building where the chief medical examiner had both his office and the three austere, sterile rooms where the various autopsies were performed. It was lunchtime and most of the personnel were gone, or at least out of sight. The entire area was eerie, the way only a place that housed the dead and their secrets could be.

But it wasn't the dead that had caused him to all but freeze in his place. In his line of work, he'd grown accustomed to seeing the dead.

The living were the ones that carried surprises with them.

And he was surprised now.

Framed in the doorway of the second autopsy room, he felt as if he'd just been catapulted back across a sea of years. Back to when he'd first walked into his bio lab in high school and had first laid eyes on her.

On Paula.

The woman in the white lab coat looked

so much like Paula, for a moment he forgot to breathe. She was as petite as Paula, who'd stood no taller than five foot four. And her coloring was almost exactly the same.

From this distance, he couldn't tell the color of her eyes, only that her hair was the same honey-brown, with reddish highlights. The woman in the room had her hair pulled back, away from her face. The last time he'd seen Paula, her hair had been long and looked as if it was in the middle of a storm. A sensuous storm that sent her hair curling in every conceivable direction.

As if sensing his presence, the woman raised her eyes and looked directly at him.

They were green.

Her eyes were green.

Like Paula's.

Chapter 3

Lucy had just made her way into the autopsy room through the rear entrance, pushing another gurney, empty this time. The gurney's last occupant, the second of the morning, had been stitched back together as reverently as possible and deposited in a steel, life-size drawer, to remain there like so much discarded memorabilia until a mortuary vehicle was dispatched to claim him. Death had been ruled accidental. The deceased was ready to go to his final resting place.

The realization that she and Dr. Daniels were not the only two breathing occupants of the room suddenly struck her.

Dr. Daniels apparently noticed it, too. Sidling up beside her, his eyes on the man in the doorway, Daniels leaned in until he had Lucy's ear and whispered, "Is it just me, or is that guy looking at you as if you were the last tall glass of cool water available to him before he has to go on a fifty-mile march?"

She wouldn't have put it that way, but now that Dr. Daniels had, Lucy had to admit that was *exactly* the way the man in the doorway was looking at her.

She felt a warmth creeping up her sides, adding color to her face. It took effort to halt its progress, but she managed. She *always* managed. It was a matter of pride with her.

The man in the doorway was dressed in civilian clothing, but there was something about his bearing that seemed to fairly shout "military" at her. Maybe it was because she'd been around so many soldiers when she was growing up, she felt she could spot a man who had military in his blood a mile away.

Now was no exception.

His dark hair was cut short and he was wearing a black leather jacket, but even so, she could see that he had shoulders so broad, they could have each served as a diving board. From what she could see, the man's waist was small, his hips taut. G.I. Joe come to life, looking as if he could fulfill every woman's fantasy.

But not hers.

The thought whispered along the perimeter of her consciousness, as if to remind her of who and what she was. And what she'd been through.

Squaring her own shoulders, Lucy stood in silence, waiting for someone else to speak. After all, eager though she was to advance both her career and her knowledge in this specific field, she was low woman on the totem pole around here. It wouldn't do for her to usurp the physician she'd been assigned to by asking the two men in the room what they were looking for.

But her more-than-healthy dose of curiosity was eating away at her.

Not to mention that she was getting exceedingly uncomfortable because Military Man's eyes hadn't left her from the moment she'd looked up. Was he trying to unnerve her for some reason? If he was, he was in for a surprise. She didn't unnerve easily. Not after the kind of life she'd led.

Luckily for her, Dr. Daniels stepped forward. "Can I help you two gentlemen?" He was all business as he looked from one man to the other, waiting for an answer.

The second of the two visitors replied. "Did you perform the autopsy on that prison transport driver who was killed?"

The inquiry startled her. Talk about coincidences, Lucy thought.

"And you would be…?" Harley pressed, looking from one to the other.

It was evident to Lucy that the doctor was not about to remotely entertain the thought of answering any questions until he had his own answered satisfactorily.

With supreme effort, Collin tore his eyes away from the woman with Paula's face and focused on the reason they were here. She looked so much like his ex-fiancée that for a moment there he'd felt as if he were coming unglued. Maybe, he told himself, after this was over, if he wasn't being sent off on another assignment, he was going to take some real time off. He had a feeling he needed it.

"Very interested in finding out information," Collin concluded the statement that the M.E. had left hanging in the air.

The doctor's small eyes moved from one man to the other. More questions presented themselves. "How did you get in here?"

Collin merely smiled. "You'd be surprised what the right badge will get you."

Unable to remain silent any longer—it simply wasn't in her nature to contain her curiosity or to hold her tongue for long—Lucy spoke up. "So far, we haven't seen any badges, right ones or wrong ones."

Damn, even her voice faintly reminded him of Paula's. Collin tried to quell the almost-jittery reaction he was feeling inside.

It was as if all his inner walls were turning to Jell-O.

Listening closer, he found more differences than similarities between the two cadences. This woman's voice, he pointed out to himself, was a bit more forceful. Paula's had always been soft, easygoing, like the woman herself.

Maybe that had been the problem, he thought. Had Paula not been as easygoing as she was, had she made some noise, maybe he would have come to his senses about his course of nonaction and done something before he'd lost her.

Reaching into the pocket of his leather jacket, Collin took out his wallet. He flipped it open and held it up for both of them to see.

"Special Ops?" the doctor read. "Army Rangers." His eyes went from the title to Collin and back again. Wiping his hands on a nearby towel, he frowned. "Why Special Ops? What is there about this case that would bring out someone like you?"

"Are you with Special Ops, too?" Lucy asked, looking at Emmett.

"FBI," Emmett corrected, taking out his own ID and showing it to both of them.

He knew he was violating several standard protocols by using his badge to get at information that he hadn't specifically been assigned to uncover, but there was no way around it. He had always believed in taking the fastest road to get somewhere. And there was no way on earth he was going to back off until he brought Jason to justice.

Besides, he knew that Ryan would never be safe until Jason was back behind bars. The man had told him during his first visit to the Double Crown Ranch that from almost the moment that Jason had escaped, letters threatening his life, his home, his family had begun coming. Letters that announced Jason's intention to kill Ryan when he least expected it. And then his wife, Lily, had been kidnapped, an event that could have ended tragically if it hadn't been for Emmett. That was a hell of a lot for a man to endure.

That Ryan Fortune hadn't gone into hiding was a testimony of the man's mettle. There was no way he would allow Jason to make good on his threat.

The doctor peered closely at the FBI credentials. "That makes a little more sense," he commented with a nod. "As a matter of fact, we had to redo the autopsy. Some kind of glitch in the system lost the records for the original so we were forced to exhume the body and perform a second autopsy. We just finished it this morning," Daniels confessed. As if suddenly making a conscious decision to be friendly, Daniels moved around Lucy and put out his hand. "Dr. Harley Daniels, M.E." Both Emmett and Collin took turns shaking it. "If you want to talk to the Chief Medical Examiner—"

Collin shook his head at the offer. "In my experience, you find out a lot more by talking to the people in the trenches."

Trenches. He even talked like a military man, Lucy thought. Once her world had been saturated with military personnel. She'd been away from that world for eight years now. Funny how being around someone she associated with the military brought all the old memories rushing back at her.

A vague sense of nostalgia drifted over her.

It almost amused Lucy, seeing as how while she was living the life, she couldn't wait to put everything associated with the military and its nomadic existence behind her. When she'd been very young, she used to fantasize that her parents would both suddenly decide to quit the military and set up housekeeping in some lovely suburban area. It didn't matter what part of the country, what mattered was that it was away from any base. She'd envisioned them taking regular nine-to-five jobs and being there with her—*for* her—at dinnertime.

She'd clung to that fantasy for more than five years. It had never materialized, but at the time, the hope that it would had been what had kept her going.

Why she suddenly found herself missing that period of her life was beyond her. Most likely it was because of the mind's tendency to romanticize the past and remember only the good.

It was also because that was the time when her mother had still been alive. Though she'd trained herself to be independent years before her mother had met her untimely fate, there were still times when she missed her mother with a fierceness that went straight down to the bone.

She became aware of Daniels looking at her. "Well, that would be us, eh, Luce? In the trenches." He sounded as if he was savoring the phrase. And then he nodded in her direction. "This is Lucy Gatling, the most promising med student we've had around here in a long time."

So that was her name, Collin said to himself. Lucy. Luce. Luz. The Spanish word for light. It suited her, he thought. He extended his hand to her. The feel of her skin was soft, almost erotic.

"And what is it that you promise?" he heard himself asking, not quite sure where the words, so unlike him, had come from.

Her eyes met his. The word *feisty* entered his mind. "Not to be flippant and put people in their place unless I really, really have to."

The response summoned a rare smile from Emmett, who had been looking at Collin as if he'd taken leave of his senses.

"What can you tell us about the autopsy?" Emmett asked, turning his attention to Daniels. "Was there anything unusual?"

"You mean, other than the fact that the driver's throat was slit so deeply it came close to severing his head clean off?"

Collin exchanged glances with Emmett. It sounded as if Jason had gone over the deep end. But then, since he had killed Christopher, they already knew that. This just reinforced their opinion.

Emmett rolled the action and its motivation over in his head. Finally he said to his new partner, "Maybe he feels he's meting out justice. Acting like judge and jury." But even as he uttered the speculation, he shook his head. He was giving Jason too much credit. More than likely, it was just an at-the-moment insane fury that had seized his brother. "I don't know. He's a hard man to pin down. Just when I think I know what makes him tick, he throws me another curve."

Maybe that was the whole point, Collin thought. His cousin was crazy. Crazy like a fox. He looked at the burly medical examiner.

"Do you know if there were any signs of a struggle? Anything at all that we could use?" Collin asked.

He was just fishing now, but you never knew when the most innocent of observations hooked up with another and eventually led somewhere. He'd learned a long time ago not to let anything pass but to examine everything, no matter how time-consuming it was. The answers that were sought could lie with the next small clue.

Daniels thought, then shrugged. "Nothing you could use."

He was chewing on something, Collin thought. "Why don't you let us be the judge of that?" he tactfully suggested.

"I haven't had the dictation transcribed into a report yet..." Daniels began.

"The dead guy had a weakness for sweets," Lucy interjected. The two men turned to look at her.

Blessed with what seemed like total recall, at least when it came to her work, she didn't need to listen to the tape recorder to refresh her memory. If it was details they were after, she could give them details.

"The guard's stomach contents showed that he had consumed several donuts not too long before he was killed."

"What else did you notice?"

Lucy glanced over her shoulder at Dr. Daniels, waiting for him to say something. She knew that she was speaking out of turn, but he just waved her on.

She didn't know if she was imagining it,

but it looked as if there was a glint of pride in the doctor's eyes, as if he were a mother bird pushing a hatchling out of the nest and watching it fly for the first time instead of sinking to the ground.

This part she felt wasn't really important, had nothing to do with the way the transport driver had died, but since she was being asked for additional information, she gave it to them.

"He would have died of liver disease before long. There was evidence of hepatitis."

The other man, the FBI agent, blew out a breath, shaking his head. "Guy should have been home, getting treatment, not out driving a prison transport," he commented.

Lucy had always been there for the underdog, maybe because a part of her identified with that role herself. "Maybe he was trying to forget the misery he saw."

The FBI agent frowned. "Nobody held a gun to his head to make him take the job."

"No," Lucy agreed, "but someone ultimately held a knife to his back."

Collin admired her grit. But it was apparently annoying Emmett. "Anything else you can recall?" Collin asked.

She nodded, having saved the best—and strangest in this case, since death had been by execution. "The oddest thing was that there was skin under his nails."

"Like he fought back?" the CIA agent asked.

"More like he tried to grab someone," Dr. Daniels put in. "Can't be sure."

"Someone," Collin echoed. Use of the word, rather than specifying Jason, pointed away from his cousin. His dark eyebrows narrowed into a single line over his nose. "You mean that the skin didn't belong to Jason?"

"That we don't know," Daniels admitted. "We don't have Jamison's DNA on file so there's no way for us to determine a match." He nodded in Lucy's direction. "She already tried."

Emmett paused, trying to remember some information he'd recently come across. Laboratory findings were not within his realm of expertise. He was a field agent. "But if you matched the skin against the DNA of, say, a blood relative, you could determine whether or not the initial DNA was in the same gene pool, right?"

"Yes," Daniels responded, "but we don't have—"

"There's that body they found in Lake Mondo," Lucy interrupted, excitement shining in her eyes, making them seem even brighter.

She hadn't been in the M.E.'s office at the time the body had surfaced, but she'd read about it. Devoured every scrap of the story. Read, too, when they had finally identified the dead man. When Jason Wilkes was captured and his true identity had come to light, the sheriff's office had tied the killer not only to Melissa Alderson's murder but also to the murder of the man who'd been found on the shores of the lake, as well.

Lucy remembered feeling sick to her stomach when she'd read that the man in custody had turned out to be the dead man's brother. That was when she'd known that Jason Jamison was a cold-blooded killer. He made her own blood run cold.

Dr. Daniels discounted her suggestion with uncertainty. "The body was pretty badly decomposed," he reminded her. There was another complication in the way, Lucy knew. The body had already been claimed and a funeral had been held. "And we would have to obtain an exhumation order from the court to dig him up before we could get any DNA to use for a test," the doctor went on. "The court doesn't exactly like issuing those."

Emmett's voice was solemn as he interrupted the discussion. "You don't have to go through anything as elaborate as having the body exhumed."

Lucy asked, "Then how…?"

Emmett's green eyes shifted in her direction. It was as if he was speaking only to her. "You can take a sample of my DNA."

Collin watched first surprise, then suspicion pass over the medical student's almost-perfect face. She was probably thinking that they were here for some ulterior purpose.

He couldn't blame her, he supposed. In her place, his mind would have probably worked the same way. But this was a time when the line about truth being stranger than fiction applied.

Lucy's eyes widened. "You're related to the escapee?" She tried to see a family resemblance, but could detect none. But then, she'd only seen one newspaper photograph of Jason Jamison.

The man barely nodded his head. "He's my brother."

Lucy's mouth nearly dropped open. She would have never guessed the two men were brothers. Talk about night and day, she thought.

Accustomed to fending for herself for a long time now, she momentarily forgot that Daniels was even in the room and that it was his place to ask the questions. "Could I see your badge again?"

Collin laughed as Emmett dug into his pocket once again. "Relax, we're not here to taint any evidence. All we want to do is find Jason and bring him in."

Putting her hand on the wallet, she looked carefully at the ID the agent provided before releasing it again. When she did, she turned toward the other man, letting her curiosity get the better of her.

"If he's the fugitive's brother, how do you figure into all this? You his sister?" She never cracked a smile.

Collin's eyes shifted toward where Daniels was standing. "She's got a flip mouth."

The doctor only laughed, his large belly shaking beneath his lab coat like a tremor building in momentum to become a major quake.

"Tell me something I don't already know." But there was nothing but fondness in his eyes as he looked at the young woman. "Lucky for her she's top notch at what she does." And then his expression sobered just a touch as the M.E. looked intently at Lucy. "You never heard me say that."

Her face was the soul of innocence as she asked, "Say what?"

"See?" Daniels looked at Collin. "What did I tell you? Top notch."

That, Collin thought, was exactly the term he would use to describe her, too.

Chapter 4

"Open wide, please. This won't hurt a bit," Lucy promised the man she now knew as Emmett Jamison. Her voice was quiet, as if she were trying to steady the nerves of a reluctant patient.

When he did as he was asked, she took the long stick and carefully swabbed the inside of his left cheek.

"I wasn't worried about the pain," Emmett told her crisply as she placed the swab in a small air-tight plastic container and sealed it.

Without realizing it, she glanced toward the other man who had stood silently by as she'd taken the necessary sample to run the test.

He read her glance and obviously took it as a solicitation for some kind of comment from him. "Sorry, he left his manners in his other coat."

His words invoked a smile from her. "But you brought yours," she said, labeling the plastic container with a black laundry marker.

"Never leave home with them."

Collin saw that his words caused Emmett's brow to furrow slightly. Emmett had always believed in the direct route, which wasn't necessarily always the polite one. The time his cousin had spent confined within the New Mexico shack that had become his hermitage had stripped him of what little social graces he'd possessed to begin with. Emmett's manner with strangers had become positively brusque and Collin had a feeling that brusque wasn't going to get them very far in this venture, especially since they weren't supposed to be walking along the trail to begin with.

"How long will the actual test to compare the two DNAs take?" Collin asked.

"If they rush it," Lucy told him, "less than a week."

It wasn't the answer he wanted, obviously, as he suppressed a belabored sigh. "That long?"

Emmett frowned, too. "Doesn't seem right in this day and age."

Taking an empty folder, Lucy made a notation on a sheet and deposited it inside the folder. "Some things don't change. No matter what progress does, it still takes nine months to have a baby."

The second the words were out of her mouth, she stopped. Lucy had no idea where that had come from. Babies were the furthest thing from her mind. Especially since she didn't intend to marry for a long time and she wasn't about to be intimate with a man until after there was a ring on her finger. A wedding ring.

As far as she could calculate, a baby wasn't going to be in her future for another nine or ten years, if then. It would probably take her that long to settle on a husband.

Right now there was no one special in her life, which was a good thing because her life was hectic enough without adding emotional conflict to it. The kind of conflict that went on when a man assumed that a relationship would just naturally progress to the next plateau. A plateau she was not about to climb to until after she was married.

She'd seen firsthand the kind of consequences that resulted when people allowed passion to govern them. She didn't need that kind of turmoil.

Lucy wondered suddenly what Military Man would have said if he knew he was in the presence of that rarest of creatures, a twenty-six-year-old virgin. Probably take it as a challenge, she mused.

It would be one challenge he wasn't going to win. She was very, very determined to remain in her present state until the right man came along and said the right words: "I do."

Since the field she was presently studying dealt exclusively with death, not birth, she had no idea where the analogy that had slipped from her lips had even come from.

What was more, she had no idea why it embarrassed her. But embarrassed she was, because she could feel the color beginning to creep up her neck, onto her cheeks again, its path heralded by a warmth that preceded it, marking the way.

Unlike her normal, take-charge self, Lucy suddenly felt hot from head to foot.

Like an amnesiac slowly becoming aware of her surroundings, she looked down at the plastic container and the cotton swab that was lodged within. Her hand tightened around it.

"Um, let me get this to the lab. The crime scene investigators already have the scrapings we took from under his fingernails." She wanted to get out of the area as quickly as possible, until the flush she felt in her cheeks had subsided and her color was back to normal. The way Military Man was looking at her, she knew he would notice. Unless he was utterly color blind.

Somehow she didn't think that was the case. She could see his lips curving into a smile as he looked at her. She began to move past him.

"You'll let us know the minute you get the results?" he pressed.

Bent on escape, Lucy began to nod her head, then suddenly stopped. She looked at Collin. "How am I supposed to get in touch with you?"

Collin grabbed a piece of paper from a desk and jotted his number on it. As he handed it to her, her fingers brushed up against his.

He knew it was crazy, but he could have sworn he felt something just then. Something electrical passing through him.

He dropped his hand to his side, nodding at the paper. "That's my cell phone number."

She glanced at the number before pocketing

the white paper, and his name, Collin. "So it is. I'd better, um…"

Lost for words, for any more of an excuse, she didn't bother finishing her statement. Instead she quickly crossed the threshold and disappeared down the twisting hallway.

"And this is my cell phone," Emmett told Daniels, handing one of his cards to the physician. "We'll be in touch," he promised, then turning on his heel, he took the same path out that Lucy had a minute earlier.

Collin had no choice but to follow. They walked quickly to the elevator bank.

Emmett's face remained without expression as he kept it forward, not sparing a glance at his cousin. "Why didn't you take a picture? It would have lasted longer."

Collin suppressed a smile. He didn't know about that. The mind was an incredible keeper of important details, as well as useless ones. The woman's face would last in his mind's eye for approximately the duration of time that he found her likeness pleasing.

He figured that would fade quickly enough. Lucy Gatling wouldn't be the first woman he was physically attracted to and she wouldn't be the last. But he could wait it out. He always had before, successfully avoiding conflicts and complications, both of which were unwanted.

"Don't know what you're talking about," Collin disavowed.

This time Emmett did look at him. And nearly jeered. "Yeah, right. The only way you could have looked any harder at that woman back there was to have taken out one of your eyeballs and handed it to her."

"Now there's a gross picture."

The bell announcing the elevator car's descent sounded. It arrived a half beat later, opening its doors. There was no one in the car.

"So is watching you become all slack-jawed over a woman in a white lab coat," Emmett countered as they walked into the elevator.

"Still don't know what you're talking about."

Emmett ignored the denial. Instead he looked at Collin, a light dawning. "Is it my imagination, or did she look a little like Paula?"

Collin felt himself stiffening the way he did just before a battle, just before the adrenaline went pumping through his veins. "Paula?"

If that was meant to be an innocent tone, it had failed miserably. They'd been friends far too long for him to be fooled by his cousin. Emmett knew, perhaps better than anyone, what Paula's walking out on him had done to Collin. Nothing messed with a man's mind more than a woman did.

"Yeah, Paula. You remember, six-years-engaged-to-you Paula," he said sarcastically, knowing that nothing more was needed than that. But just in case, he added, "The one who married someone you called your best friend."

"He *was* my best friend," Collin confirmed quietly as they stepped out of the elevator again and began to walk toward the front entrance. "He took care of Paula every time I was away on assignments. Couldn't expect her to sit home four, five weeks at a time while I was taking care of business."

Taking care of business. It was a euphemistic way of describing what he'd done for a living. What he still did. Infiltrating drug cultures in South America, crossing borders in European countries that were so close together they could have been opposite walls of a medium-size closet, all while tracking down a fugitive who was increasingly becoming desperate.

Not unlike what he was setting out to do now, he thought.

"Paula was young." He continued his defense of the woman he figured he was always destined to remain in love with. "She wanted a good time."

Emmett laughed shortly. There was no sign of humor on his mouth and his eyes were flat. In this case, he took umbrage for his cousin even if Collin wouldn't take it for himself. "And good old William certainly gave it to her, didn't he?"

Collin refused to think about that. Going there served no purpose. She was married and that was that. "Bottom line, he made her happy. I didn't."

Emmett's frown became deep enough to bury pirate treasure in. "Don't act like it doesn't bother you, Collin."

"It did," he admitted, then shrugged good-naturedly, wanting the subject to be dropped, "but it's over and I learned a lesson from it."

Emmett spared him a side glance as they walked to the car. "Which was?"

"That I'm not cut out to maintain something that needs constant care, constant watching. Constant nurturing." And that was what marriage was, something that needed continuous work. He was never around long enough to put in the hours.

The denial sounded too pat to Emmett. "Is that what was going through your head while you were looking at Ms. Med Student and drooling?"

The image of himself as a lovesick puppy was enough to almost make him laugh out loud. "No drooling was involved. I was just surprised that there could be two women who looked so much alike."

"Looks, yeah," Emmett conceded, "but once she opened her mouth, that woman was no Paula. This one's got a head on her shoulders."

They went down another row of cars. "It'd be better if it was on her neck."

Emmett shook his head, a smile peeling back his lips. "You always were the only one who could ever make me laugh."

"I was the only one who ever tried," Collin pointed out. He stopped to look around and finally spotted Emmett's car two aisles over. He motioned the man to follow him as he lengthened his stride. "Let's go to the hospital and see if the other driver is back among the living yet."

Emmett nodded. He'd already decided on that course of action himself. "That's why we work so well together, Collin. We think alike."

"No, we don't," Collin denied, reaching the vehicle first. He waited for Emmett to unlock it. "You just like to take the credit for my ideas."

Putting his key in the lock, Emmett laughed. It was good being around Collin again. He'd forgotten what it felt like to interact with his cousin. Forgotten what it was like to feel human again.

Or as close to human as he could manage, under the circumstances.

The policeman whose job it was to guard the comatose prison transport driver looked as if he'd sent his brain out for the afternoon so as not to succumb to the mind-numbing task. He sat on a chair, tilting the rear legs so that the front ones were off the floor, his chair balanced against the wall. An unread magazine was spread over his lap and the officer was staring off into oblivion when they came on the floor.

The sound of footsteps had him turning around and nearly pitching off his chair. He recovered himself at the last moment, rising to his feet.

"You can't go in there," he announced, his voice a great deal deeper than would have been expected, given his shallow physique. Collin suspected that the man was lowering it for effect and didn't normally speak in that timbre.

Emmett gave the policeman a dark look and then flashed his credentials. He glanced toward Collin, who followed suit. The policeman read both with great interest. Collin could almost hear him saying, "Wow."

The officer's Adam's apple, rather prominent, danced a little as it went up and down. He nodded his head at both IDs almost as if he was paying homage to them.

"I'm sorry, no one told me you were coming to see the driver."

Emmett awarded him with one of his frostier looks. "Why should they?"

"Um, that is…" The officer's voice trailed off as he looked completely at a loss for words or any sort of an adequate reply.

"Taking no prisoners today?" Collin asked his cousin as they walked into the room.

"Not today," Emmett confirmed. There was nothing he detested more than incompetence, even if it worked in his favor.

Collin eased the door closed behind them.

The small, single-bed room looked not unlike a mini-intensive care unit with machines surrounding the comatose transporter's bed. There was a constant hum in the room so that no one entering it would, even for a moment, forget the existence of the various machines and how much they were needed to keep the man hooked up to them alive. For now.

Collin approached the bed, studying the face of the man he'd hoped had regained consciousness by now. The transporter, a man for whom the term "average" might have been coined if describing his hair, height and appearance, now sported a pasty complexion. He looked like a man who'd been on the brink of death and was even now still very much tottering on the edge. His fate, despite the noble efforts of a team of surgeons who'd kept him under for five hours, working feverishly in hopes of negating the damage that had been done by the stab wounds, had not yet been decided.

They could lose him at any minute.

Collin willed the victim's eyes to open.

They didn't.

Feeling unusually frustrated, he looked at the machine that monitored the patient's vital signs. His pulse, blood pressure and respiration gauges were all making the appropriate, comforting beeping noises. Across the screen colorful wavy lines snaked their way from one end to the other, sometimes uniformly, sometimes jaggedly, with a regularity that provided the information that the man was still hanging on. Still fighting.

He should have been dead. Like his partner. And yet, he wasn't.

Collin picked up the chart that was already full and glanced over it. He knew enough medical terminology to get by as long as it didn't get too involved.

"Human spirit's an incredible thing," he commented, flipping the pages back again. "According to this—" he indicated the chart that he replaced at the foot of the driver's bed "—this man should have been dead. The knife obviously had a long blade. It went through his back and was inches shy of his lungs. If it had been just a little over, he would have already been six feet in the ground."

Emmett studied the man in silence for a moment, looking beyond the inert figure. Visualizing the scene that might have taken place in the transport vehicle. Had they hit a ditch, causing the driver to lose control of the bus? There'd been no blowout, so that wasn't the cause of the change of fortune within the vehicle.

What had happened inside the van to turn the prisoner into the jailer?

Without fully realizing it, he voiced his thoughts out loud. "Wonder if he turned and made a run for it at the last second, not like the guy in the coroner's office who was caught by surprise."

Collin hadn't made up his mind yet; there wasn't enough evidence to spin a theory. "Well, something's different about him, or else he'd be in a steel drawer, right next to his buddy." He rolled the last word around in his mouth. "Think they were friends?" He raised his eyes to Emmett, answering his own question when his cousin made no response. "I guess that depends on if they worked together on a regular basis. Most people usually develop some kind of relationship if they work together." Unless they were in his line of work, he added silently. In the field, there was never enough time to do anything except think about staying alive.

"I don't," Emmett retorted crisply.

"I said 'most.'" He laughed shortly. "You're not like most people, Emmett. Most people, if they get fed up with their job, take a vacation. They don't take a powder and retreat from the world the way you did."

As Collin spoke, his tone deceptively light, he continued studying the unconscious man in the bed. Trying to see himself in his skin. Had he felt panic at the last moment? Had he looked down the blade of the knife as it had gone in? Seen his partner die? He wondered if there was a way he could get inside the transport vehicle and look around. "You were that type that Thoreau used to write about, the one who marches to a different drummer."

Emmett's expression gave nothing away. Not even if he took offense at the description or saw it as a compliment. "I wouldn't exactly say what you do for a living is run of the mill."

Collin's mouth curved. Listening, he caught what he felt was just the slightest defensive note in Emmett's voice. "Maybe we have the same drummer."

Emmett inclined his head, as if letting the matter go. "Maybe."

Collin's eyes narrowed as he moved the sheet aside to look at the driver's forearms that were tucked beneath the covers. His cousin was at the foot of the bed, going over the medical chart on his own and frowning deeply. "Hey, Emmett, take a look at this."

With a disgusted sigh, Emmett replaced the chart. It was pretty much all Greek to him. "What?"

Standing back, Collin indicated what had

caught his eye. "This scratch on his hand."
Emmett rounded the bed and came over to
where Collin was standing.

Collin looked at Emmett. "Are you thinking what I'm thinking?"

Slowly, Emmett nodded his head, his eyes
still on the single short, jagged scratch on top
of the man's hand. "That either the attending
physician or nurse was pretty damn clumsy
with the IV needle or someone scratched this
man during a struggle."

Collin thought of the other driver. The medical student had said there'd been skin under
his nails. "Maybe we should have someone
take a sample of this guy's DNA and see if
it matches what they found under the other
guy's nails."

Emmett continued to stare at the patient.
Like a Greek chorus, the machines went on
humming in the background. "You thinking
they might have fought? You think that's why
Jason got the chance to get the drop on them
and escape?"

Collin wasn't really sure where his thoughts
were going here. There still wasn't enough
to build a theory. He felt like he was trying
to paint a portrait without the benefit of any
lighting to guide his strokes.

"Maybe it's a long shot." He nodded at the man in the bed. "Maybe this guy had an overly enthusiastic bed partner before he came on the job that morning and it's just a coincidence." He sighed, dragging his hand through his hair. "But right now everything's a mystery, so we might as well gather up as many pieces of the puzzle as we can to see how and if they fit together and what kind of a picture we come up with."

Emmett frowned. Being with the FBI had left him a stickler for protocol and going by the book. "We're already here against orders. Taking this guy's DNA violates his rights."

Fine points like that had never bothered Collin. They had little meaning for a man who'd had to live from moment to moment, always harboring the knowledge that his next breath might be his last.

Collin shook his head. "You're thinking trial, Emmett. I'm thinking tracking down Jason. That's why we're both here, right? Whether or not this guy was just in the wrong place at the wrong time, or for some reason was responsible for Jason making good his escape, is something we don't know yet, might not ever know if he dies. But we can find out if he's the guy that the other transporter scratched. That's something concrete."

"But why would he scratch him? Why him and not Jason?" Emmett threw the question out for speculation.

Collin shrugged, another theory forming. "Maybe this guy was in on it. Maybe Jason bribed him and he was trying to hold the other guy down so that Jason could stab him a few more times and make sure he was dead."

"Or maybe the other guy was trying to shove him out of the way, trying to escape from Jason." Which meant that neither guard was in on it. That was an unusually optimistic take on the subject, given Emmett's usual black outlook on things.

Collin smiled. "Yeah, there's that, too. First, let's find out if he did scratch him. Then we'll work on why."

They had no facilities available to them except for the ones they were already using. "Back to the M.E.'s office."

Collin grinned. "You read my mind."

Emmett snorted. "Not very heavy reading."

Collin opened the door, letting him walk out first. "Never claimed it was."

Chapter 5

It felt as if the dampness was seeping into his very bones. Sheltered from the elements, Jason was still a long way from being warm. He pulled the sheepskin jacket closer to him, shivering as he sat deep within the bowels of the cave he'd staked out.

Damn it, it wasn't supposed to turn out this way. He wasn't supposed to be hiding out in a cave like some kind of common criminal.

Rage bubbled up inside him like so much lava waiting to spew out.

There wasn't anything common about him, he thought angrily. He was better than all of them. Better than Ryan Fortune, certainly better than his brother, or that bitch he'd wound up strangling in a fit of rage.

That was her own fault.

Melissa's face sprang up in front of his mind's eye. His breathing became audible, echoing within the cavernous walls. She had pushed him to it. Almost dared him to do it, dared him to silence her taunts as she'd flung them at him with reckless aplomb.

Served her right.

He'd known from the start what he was dealing with. Known, too, that she was expendable. Everyone was expendable as far as he was concerned, just as long as he reached his goal.

It hurt his gut to admit it, but somewhere along the line, he'd developed…well, not feelings for her exactly. But there'd been a sort of kinship between them. A commonality of soul. They'd been two people dealt the wrong hand by the whimsical gods of fate, bent on righting that wrong.

Somewhere along the line he'd begun to think that Melissa was after the same thing he was and that she would be willing to share his triumph once he'd reached it. Instead she'd gone after his target. Made a cheap play for the man because she'd wanted to become the fourth Mrs. Ryan Fortune.

The thankless, heartless bitch.

Jason had no doubt that she would have told Fortune everything about him, about his intricate plot to bring the man down, the fact that he'd killed Christopher who tried to stop him, *everything*. Just to further her own cause. To ingratiate herself to Fortune.

Without so much as a backward glance, she would have sold him out.

After everything he'd done for her.

So he'd killed her.

When he'd pulled her into the room on the secluded second floor of Steven Fortune's mansion, during a party honoring Ryan, part of him knew she was never going to leave it alive. She'd begun to rail at him, calling him a loser, saying he was going to wind up just like his grandfather Farley and that she should have never hooked up with him.

Something had snapped inside of him. He'd gone almost on automatic pilot, stepping back and watching himself wrap his hand around her throat to squeeze the very life out of her, bit by bit.

Unfortunately for him, someone else had watched him squeeze the life out of her, too.

A damn investigative reporter of all people. When Natalie McCabe saw him strangle Melissa, she'd reported it to Steven Fortune—and to two detectives who were at the party.

He'd wound up being arrested at the very party where he'd meant to make an even greater impression on Ryan Fortune.

To add insult to injury, those bungling two-bit toy cops in Red Rock had somehow managed to connect him to Christopher's murder, as well. He had never thought that he'd be caught for either of his crimes. Incarceration was for little men, not for him. But somehow he'd wound up in prison orange, handcuffed and shackled like some kind of animal instead of being regaled as the brilliant strategist that he was.

Down, but not out.

Never out.

The money he'd managed to get from an underling at Fortune TX, Ltd. had helped him buy his escape. When his lawyer had told him he was going to be transported to a maximum security prison, he knew his chance had come. It had taken very little to bribe the main transport guard.

He'd seen more light coming out of a 15-watt bulb than he'd witnessed in the man's eyes. But they'd lit up fast enough when he'd mentioned money. He'd made the deal, asking the Neanderthal to help him escape, never giving him the full details of what he'd planned to do the moment he was uncuffed. Initially he'd placated the guard's uneasiness by saying that he was to knock the driver out and then unlock his handcuffs. He'd never said a word to the guard that he intended to kill the driver. Certainly never mentioned that after he'd killed the one, he was going to get rid of him, as well.

Dead men told no tales, right? The old pirate adage was as true now as it had been when pirate ships roamed the seven seas.

He'd gotten a sensational rush executing the driver. Envisioning Ryan in front of him, he'd slit the man's throat from ear to ear. The death rattle he heard had sent his adrenaline singing.

McGruder had panicked, crying that no one was supposed to have been killed.

Which was when he'd turned the knife the guard had hidden for him on the van and driven it into the man's chest. Twice.

McGruder had dropped like a lead weight right in front of him, his face frozen for all eternity in startled surprise.

Or so he'd thought.

McGruder should have been dead, just like that driver. So why wasn't he?

Jason clenched his cold hands in angry, impotent fists and held them tightly against himself, battling an overwhelming rage.

When he'd ventured out of the cave where he was holed up to get provisions for himself, the first thing he'd taken note of was the discarded newspaper on the bench. The headline had been devoted to him. The article began by declaring his "daring escape" and the death of one of the transport guards.

One of the transport guards.

Which meant that the other was still alive. A second headline, smaller and over the last column on the right, told him that far from pushing up daisies, the man who had aided him had been taken to a nearby hospital and was presently in a coma.

A coma, for God's sakes!

McGruder should have been dead.

He was *going* to be dead. As soon as he could safely make the right arrangements. There was no way he trusted fate to tie up this loose end for him, even though according to what he could read quickly without arousing suspicion, the wounded man was not expected to pull through.

The man had to have a charmed life just to have made it this far, Jason grumbled, massaging his arms to create the feeling of some kind of warmth.

But when it came to charmed lives, there was no disputing that he was the champion. And he meant it to remain that way.

He also meant to eliminate his primary target, the reason this entire charade of his being a rising young executive at Fortune TX, Ltd. had taken place. He'd already been beyond fed up with the part when his cover was blown. But he was still going to wipe all traces of Ryan Fortune, his family and their influence off the face of the earth even if it took him a lifetime.

It would have made his grandfather proud.

The thought heartened him. Farley and his stories were the only part of his childhood that he looked back upon with any sort of fondness.

His plan all set in his mind, Jason began to riffle through the plastic shopping bag, taking out the provisions he'd brought back with him. It was way past time for breakfast and his stomach was growling, making him even more surly than he already was.

"I didn't expect to see you again today. It's too soon, you know. There's no answer yet,"

Lucy tagged on after she'd gotten over her initial surprise at seeing that the two men she'd met this morning were back.

This time she was alone in the autopsy area. The unexpected rush was over. The autopsies, all done, all dictated, were just waiting for transcription. She was busy cataloging tissue samples that had to go to the lab.

Lucy had assumed that their visit to the hospital, which Daniels had overheard was the men's next destination this morning, couldn't have been very fruitful. After all, the other guard couldn't tell them anything in his present state.

But there had to be a hundred other clues they could be running down right about now, separately or together. Why were they back here again?

"We didn't come about the DNA results," Collin told her, taking the lead when Emmett said nothing. He'd always considered himself rather closemouthed. Compared to Emmett, he was a regular chatterbox. "We came to ask you to take another sample to run."

Lucy looked from Collin to Emmett, confused. "Why? There was nothing wrong with the first one."

"No, not from him," Collin told her. "From someone else."

She put down the pen she was writing with. "Who?"

"The other guard."

She stared at Collin. "The one who's still in a coma?"

Collin nodded solemnly, looking around the room. It made him think of the inside of a stainless-steel refrigerator. "That's the one."

"I'm not that up on my law, but isn't that illegal?"

"You let us worry about the legal points." Emmett's voice was sharp, curt, cutting off any further comment on her part.

But the way he said it only served to arouse her suspicions. Up until now she'd only been kidding. However something just didn't feel right. And when it didn't feel right, it usually meant that it wasn't. She'd learned to trust her instincts a long time ago. They were rarely wrong.

Lucy paused for a long moment, looking from one man to the other, trying to gauge their motivation and whether or not she should make a run for it. If they were dangerous for some reason, she didn't want to be alone with them.

But Collin didn't look dangerous, she thought. Just somber. She could handle somber; dangerous was something else again. Summoning bravado, she looked directly at him. "Those credentials you showed me were real, right?"

"You can call and check with the Bureau and the Agency," Collin told her. "We are who we say we are."

Lucy hesitated. She was somewhat familiar with lies that passed for the truth. She'd used them herself during her teen years. Living for several years with her grandmother, she was unaccustomed to having any real authority over her. She would come and go as she pleased. When it came her mother's or her father's turn to house her, she'd get around their questions and their rules by learning how to phrase her responses so that it sounded as if she was in agreement or planned to live up to whatever it was that they expected of her. Spin, she'd discovered, meant everything.

Right now she had a feeling she was being spun herself.

She looked pointedly at Collin. "And will they also tell me that those two people who you are supposed to be are currently supposed be *here,* investigating this prison escape?"

Collin smiled to himself. She was sharp. He'd always liked a sharp mind. To him it was as sexy as a long pair of legs, which she also seemed to possess despite her overall petite stature. The straight, dark skirt she wore along with her lab coat was short enough to make her legs look endless.

It was also enough to stir him even though he didn't want to be.

"It's not for you to question us," Emmett informed her curtly.

Collin caught his cousin's eye and shook his head slowly. Intimidation might have been the right way to go at the hospital with the wet-be-hind-the-ears police officer, but that wasn't the case here. Not with Lucy Gatling. From what he could ascertain, the woman was too sharp, too savvy, too inclined to ask the right questions of the wrong people and thereby arouse suspicion.

They needed her on their side, Collin decided. And she had to move there of her own volition, not through any coercion on their part.

Far more acquainted with force than gentility, Collin still managed to gently take her by the arm and usher the med student over to the side. Away from Emmett.

He lowered his voice and spoke confidentially, hoping that might arouse a feeling of camaraderie within her. "Look, we need your help."

She was right. Something *was* wrong here. "I can't just—"

Collin cut her off before she could complete her protest. He needed to appeal to the feminine side of her before the iron curtain came down. He had a feeling that she could wield her logical side with aplomb, and though they needed her expertise, it was her empathy that would best help them.

"Emmett really is with the FBI and I'm really with Special Ops," he told her. "And," he added, "Emmett really is Jason Jamison's younger brother." His eyes held hers, silently making his appeal. "This is an in-family thing. I don't know if you're familiar with the details of the case—"

With anyone else, Lucy would have taken the words as patronizing. But the look in his eyes told her that he was asking a genuine question. And speaking to her as if she were his equal. "I've read a couple of newspaper articles," she replied.

He nodded. "Then you know that Jason is probably insane. Emmett and I want to track him down and find him before he hurts anyone else."

"Isn't that what everyone on the case is trying to do?"

"Yeah, but he's not everyone's brother," he pointed out. Which made this all personal. "And we want to take him in alive if possible."

She looked at him for a long moment. "Exactly how are you involved in this?"

"I'm Jason's cousin. More important than that, I'm Emmett's cousin." His tone was frank, honest. Instincts told him that she would respect nothing less. Respond to nothing less. "My name is Lt. Collin Jamison." He nodded toward Emmett. "He asked for my help."

In all her dealings with the military, she'd never met a ranger before. Members of that group were regarded as elite. A little above human. He looked very human to her. "And you really are with Special Ops?"

He grinned at her, making her stomach unexpectedly flip over like a pancake on a frying pan. "After this is over, we can go camping and I'll show you my survival skills."

She laughed and shook her head. The man had a charm about him, there was no denying that. Added to his chiseled features and his almost-heart-stopping physique with its hard muscles and rigid structure and it was a combination that was difficult to resist. She had more than a sneaking suspicion that Collin Jamison got his way not just through skill, but because of his looks.

Lucy glanced over her shoulder at the other man. Emmett's impatience was all but wafting over to her like heat emanating from a concrete wall in the dead of summer. From here on in, she had a gut feeling she was going to be going against the rules. It gave her pause. She had a lot to lose.

But then, she had always been a risk taker. Her mother's death had taught her only one thing. That life was tenuous. You might as well live it to the fullest if you could.

"All right," she said to Collin, "what is it that you want from me?"

From out of the depths of his soul, long-buried emotions that he had begun to think he'd only imagined or dreamed whispered responses to her question that luckily did not reach his lips. She aroused him. Partially because she reminded him of Paula, partially because she did Paula one better. She had a verve, a wit to her that Paula hadn't.

He could see himself holding Lucy in his arms. Could almost taste the texture of her lips against his. Could feel his body responding to the fantasy that was spinning itself in his head.

It took effort to mentally pour cold water on it. But he managed. Just barely.

"The other guard's still unconscious in the hospital," he told her. "There are scratches on the inside of his right forearm. You found skin and blood under the dead man's nails. We'd like you to take a sample of the guard's DNA and compare it to what you have."

Her brow furrowed as she tried to fill in the empty spaces. "So now you think that one guard fought with the other?"

He inclined his head. "Something like that."

She didn't quite follow the logic of this. "What good will knowing that do you?" Before Collin answered, she hurried to add, "I'm not trying to be obstinate, I'm serious. I want to know. I'm going into forensic medicine as my career and I want all the insight I can get."

He blew out a breath. He knew that Emmett thought they were wasting time here, but he felt she had a right to an answer. He wished he had one.

"To be honest, I don't know yet. It'll show us that the two prison guards fought. Which could mean that they just didn't get along, or, most likely, that at least one of them was being bribed by Jason to help him escape.

"It's the only thing that makes sense," he allowed. "Jason couldn't have just pulled this off on his own. He had to have some kind of help." He let her in on a miscellaneous piece of information he'd picked up on the way over. "No one reported any clothes missing within fifteen miles of where they found the van. I doubt if Jason's running around in a bright orange jumpsuit, since that makes him a hell of a hard thing to ignore.

"And if he didn't steal any clothes, then someone brought some onto the van and hid them for him. Which means he had an accomplice. And more than likely, his accomplice was one of the guards. Or both." And then he shrugged. "It's the best we can come up with until the guard wakes up."

"*If* the guard wakes up," Emmett interjected from the sidelines.

"Always the optimist," Collin murmured, but he said it with affection.

Growing up, their lives had been as different as butterflies were from earthworms. There'd been a great deal of turmoil in Emmett's life when he was growing up. Unlike either Emmett's or Jason's, his own childhood had been tranquil and happy. He'd had a healthy relationship with his own father, August, a psychologist who worked for the CIA.

He'd admired his father so much that when it came to choosing the path he wanted to take for the rest of his life, he'd majored in psychology and had gone to West Point to be a soldier like his father had been. The CIA Special Ops program had seemed like the natural step for him after graduation.

Still speaking to Lucy, Collin inclined his head toward his cousin. "What he said." And then he looked at her with eyes that seemed to see into her very soul. "Will you help us?"

Lucy blew out a breath, then lifted the hair off her neck, the way she did whenever she was debating something that left her feeling uncertain.

This would mean stepping outside the lines, something that was bound to get her in trouble if she was discovered. She wasn't anywhere in her career where she could risk censure or the displeasure of the powers that be. Still, she could empathize with the two men. Knew how frustrating it could be to be told to stand on the sidelines when a member of your own family was involved. To this day, she still had no clue how her mother had died or why.

The nebulous "in the line of duty" covered a great deal and explained absolutely nothing. But whenever she asked for details, she received no answers.

"Okay," she finally said, throwing her lot in with Military Man and his solemn cousin. "I have to take care of some tissue samples first, but after that I'm supposed to go to lunch. I guess I could try hospital cafeteria food for a change of pace."

She was rewarded with a grin from Collin. Like a shot, it went straight to her knees, weakening them as if they'd been physically hit.

With his killer smile and charm, he was going to be one to watch out for, she suddenly thought. She'd be better off having dealings with his cousin. Although good-looking, the man scowled enough to take the place of a rain cloud at a moment's notice.

At least that gave her a fighting chance. She had an uneasy feeling that being around Lt. Collin Jamison left her with no chance at all. Even though she'd only met him, she'd a feeling that he could pose a threat to life as she knew it. And turn it on its ear with very little effort at all.

Chapter 6

The same officer was sitting in front of the transport guard's room when Collin returned to the hospital with Lucy. It didn't take a body-language expert to see that the young police-man was even more bored now than he had been this morning.

He had all the signs of someone starved for action, Collin thought. The officer came to life the moment he saw the two of them walking toward him, immediately jumping to his feet. The chair he'd been tilting on started to fall over but he grabbed it and set it straight before it could hit the floor.

Collin smiled at the guard as if they were

old friends. That confused the hell out of him, Collin thought, judging by the man's expression.

"I'm going to have to impose on you one more time, Officer Harris."

The slight pause between the statement and the policeman's surname was hardly perceptible as he read the man's badge. But Lucy had heard it and she glanced at the man at her side with interest. He read people rather than just stomped right into the middle of things the way so many of her parents' friends had. She supposed it was all in keeping with the image of "the new soldier" the military was trying to push, she thought, doing her best to suppress a smile. She wondered how her father would have reacted to him once the initial approval of a man in uniform had faded a little.

The police officer looked a little leery. He glanced up and down the hall, but no one else was coming their way. Lucy couldn't decide whether that fact relieved him or made him nervous.

"With all due respect, sir," he said to Collin after a moment's hesitation, "this isn't supposed to be Grand Central Station."

In Collin's experience, usually only New York natives referred to busy areas that way.

He'd *thought* he'd detected a hint of an accent. He smiled, ignoring the intent of the statement and diverting the conversation to a path of his choosing. "From New York?"

The officer looked surprised at having been found out. He cleared his throat uncertainly. "A long time ago." The next words were uttered with a thick Texas twang that he purposely laid on with broad strokes. "Came here with my folks when I was ten."

Collin nodded, absorbing the personal information with a degree of satisfaction. Things were always easier when the people he was dealing with took on names and backgrounds, when they unwittingly shared a little of themselves, however minor. Doing so brought them all up to a completely different plateau. A plateau where secrets were less dear and things that he needed to know were more accessible.

Harris cleared his throat again. "You're the first one to guess that I'm from New York." It seemed important for him to let them know that.

Collin sincerely doubted that. But with an indulgent nod of his head, he did his best to make the young policeman feel better, since it seemed to matter to him. "I've got a good ear for accents, even if they're slight." Still, the officer looked disappointed to be placed so easily. He needed the officer buoyed, not crestfallen. "Otherwise I would have never heard it." He turned toward Lucy. "Officer Harris, Dr. Gatling is with the coroner's office and she needs to see the man in that room."

Harris glanced at the ID tag that hung halfway down her chest, held in place with a navy-blue chord. "Kind of ghoulish, isn't it?" The police officer frowned. "Seeing as how he's not dead yet."

"We're not jumping the gun," Collin assured him. "We just need a couple of minutes alone with him to rule something out." He tossed the words over his shoulder toward Harris as he opened the door.

Quickly he ushered Lucy in ahead of him and shut the door.

The sound of machines working in harmony echoed through the room. Lucy turned on her heel to look at the man who had brought her here. About to say something, she let it go in favor of something lighter. "You promoted me."

"Excuse me?"

After the morgue and the autopsy area, this room seemed full of life, even though Mc-Gruder's case was still touch and go. "You just called me *Dr.* Gatling back there. According to you, I just sailed through my final year and graduation."

His smile was sexy, working its way under her skin twice as fast because he didn't seem to be aware of it. "And I'm sure you will."

She was nothing if not intelligent. The very way she held herself told him that she believed it, too. But he wasn't here to analyze her body, awe-inspiring though it was. His job was to round up Jason and the faster the better. Every moment they delayed was a moment's opportunity forever lost.

"Now, about that DNA sample…" he prodded, glancing over his shoulder at the closed door.

He had no idea how long they would remain alone in the room. A nurse or doctor could come through those doors at any moment, or worse, someone from one of the agencies involved in the investigation could be coming by to check on McGruder even now.

They needed to hurry.

Lucy nodded. Slipping on plastic gloves she'd put in her coat pocket, she took out a pair of tweezers and got to work. Leaning over the unconscious guard, she plucked out a hair and held it aloft to examine it.

Collin looked at it from his vantage point, but saw nothing. His eye wasn't trained for it. "What are you looking for?"

"Just making sure it has a root attached." She looked at him with a smile. "It does and it'll do fine."

He glanced at his watch. Luck had a way of holding up for so long and then evaporating. No one had found them on his first trip here and they were still home free on their second visit. But how much longer? "Anything else you need?"

"Probably my head examined for doing this," Lucy muttered under her breath, placing the single hair into a small plastic envelope. She sealed it, then tucked it into her purse. "We're done."

Not soon enough for him. He was beginning to get a pins-and-needles feeling at the back of his neck the way he always did when something was in danger of going wrong. He needed her out of here before anyone asked any questions and realized that they were acting independent of any particular directive from the variety of bureaus and departments vying for primary jurisdiction over the case.

"Let's go."

He didn't have to tell her twice. Adrenaline

had been rushing through her veins from the moment they'd stepped onto the floor, even though she was fighting to keep a blasé expression in place. It wasn't all that easy to maintain, seeing as how her heart was pounding in her throat.

Lucy hadn't been kidding about the head examination she was contemplating. By all rights, she shouldn't be here. If she was as straight an arrow as her mother had been, she would have probably called someone in the Army Rangers to report Collin's misconduct.

But that dilemma had been taken out of her hands the moment she'd agreed to go along with this. Despite her feelings about intimacy before marriage, moral righteousness had never been a problem for her. She always did the right thing—the way she saw it. And this, in its own way, was right.

Besides, doing this put an exciting edge to what had heretofore been a very by-the-numbers assignment. Not that the actual case was. But her participation in it had been. Boring to the extreme.

Until now.

She nodded at the police officer as they left the room again. Military Man said something to him in parting that brought out a smile from the young man, but it was all a buzz in her ears right now.

As the extremely masculine lieutenant hustled her to the elevator, his hand pressed against the small of her back indicating that her pace wasn't quick enough to satisfy his needs, Lucy could vaguely understand what it was that her mother had felt. Taking on assignments that dropped her off somewhere in one of the four corners of the world, demanding that she live by her wits and her skill. It was one hell of an exciting rush, she had to say that for it.

In a way, she'd never felt closer to her mother than she did right at this moment.

And, in an odd way, close to this man she hadn't even known existed a short twenty-four hours ago.

They were the only occupants when the elevator swallowed them up and began its descent to the first floor. Only after the doors closed did Lucy allow herself to relax a little. She leaned against the wall and breathed a sign of relief.

She saw a look of concern pass over Military Man's face. "You all right?"

She hadn't realized that she was so audible. Lucy flushed, straightening. She did her best to pretend as if this was commonplace to her instead of something she'd never done before. She couldn't remember ever crossing a higher authority than that belonging to either one of her parents.

"Fine." And then she couldn't help adding with a laugh, "For a woman who might have just seen her career go down the tubes."

"No tubes," he guaranteed with a shake of his head. "And if anything comes up, it was my fault. I made you do it."

So, he was willing to take the blame for this. Very gallant of him. She liked that. Lucy smiled. "No one who knows me would ever believe you."

He cocked his head as he studied her. So he wasn't wrong about that spirit he saw in her eyes. "You that stubborn?"

"I've been known to be." She looked up and saw the red numbers drift by slowly, like snowflakes falling to earth. "The point is, Lieutenant, no one makes me do what I don't want to."

He had no doubts of that. Collin crossed his arms in front of him. "So why are you helping me?"

"Because I like puzzles." That was the intellectual answer, but there was far more to it than that. After a beat, she told him the primary reason. "Because the look on your cousin's face got to me."

Collin's own look was rather dubious. "You talking about his scowl?"

She shook her head. "Maybe I should amend that to say the look in your cousin's eyes. I saw a look like that on an orphan's face once." And it had never left her. It made her pray never to feel that alone, that sad. "It was on the news. He was from one of those war-besieged countries. His home had just gotten bombed, killing his entire family. He was all he had left in the world." Pausing, she looked up at Collin. "But then, your cousin has you, doesn't he?"

"Yeah, he does." And his sense of family was right up there with God and Country. Maybe he felt the way he did about God and Country because of the sense of family his father had instilled in him.

The elevator came to a stop on the ground floor, its gunmetal doors opening slowly. Collin stepped out, taking her elbow as if to guide her toward the front entrance.

Lucy deliberately pulled her elbow away. Her eyes met his. "I've been walking on my own now for a number of years, Lieutenant. I've gotten pretty good at it, too."

It was all part of his habit of taking charge. The more he controlled, the better the chance that everything would go his way.

He made a show of dropping his hand to his side. "Sorry, didn't mean to usurp your autonomy," he told her. "Habit. Out in the field, when every second could be your last, you find yourself becoming a bit of a control freak."

She thought of her parents. Not so much her father, but when her mother was alive, it had been a constant struggle for independence whenever she was at home. Her father had learned early on that she was every bit as stubborn, as headstrong as her mother and that he was a poor match for either.

"Yes, I know."

The pregnant tone had him looking at her quizzically. "You in the military?"

"Everything but sworn in," she quipped. And then, because she could see the questions in his eyes, she added, "Both my parents wore the uniform."

"What branch?"

Lucy hurried to match his stride as they followed the exit signs down one corridor after another. "Army. Like you."

He stopped short of the exit, allowing her to walk out first as the doors yawned open.

Standing outside for a moment, he took a deep breath. Cold air swirled into his lungs. It smelled and felt as if they might be in for a snowstorm. Collin looked around at the people as they passed them on the street, all wrapped up in their own worlds.

Sometimes, he thought, it was more dangerous out here in civilization than it was in a war zone. At least in an officially declared war zone, you knew more or less where you stood, who your enemies were. Out here, you never knew who might be out to get you. Who would have ever thought, when they were growing up together, that Jason would have turned out to be such a threat? That he was capable of turning on everyone? Capable of murdering his own brother as well as who knew how many others. There were three bodies with Jason's mark on them. Would they find more if they looked? Civilization, with its inability to read beneath the surface, had helped Jason to hide his cunning.

Hell of a bitter pill for his uncle Blake to swallow, he thought.

Lucy spotted the car they'd used parked where they'd left it, across the street in an adjacent lot. "We'd better get this to the lab," she prompted.

Since the results would be back in a matter of days, not hours, he saw no reason to rush now that they were out of the hospital. "I owe you lunch."

She was surprised that he remembered the throwaway comment he'd made earlier. She also remembered the rest of that offer and puckered her face. "Hospital food? I'll pass, thanks."

He laughed. She looked adorable just then. Impish. He found himself fighting back a strong desire to kiss her. There was no getting away from the fact that he felt attracted to this woman who reminded him of Paula and yet didn't. "I was thinking of a real restaurant."

Lucy pushed her sleeve up her wrist and glanced at her watch. "It'll have to be a fast one. I'm due back soon."

He could appreciate the lack of time. Emmett was out there, following up leads, and could use a hand. But still, an obligation was an obligation. And he'd promised to feed her.

"How about over there?" Collin pointed to a sandwich shop, one of a chain that was popping up all over the state. This one was in the middle of the block across the street.

Breakfast had been a piece of toast, burned on one end because of a defective toaster. Given that she didn't care for charcoal, she'd left that part untouched. She was hungry and saw no point in denying that fact. "Sounds good to me."

The light turned green. Collin began to take her elbow as they started to cross the street, then pulled back his hand, holding it and the other one up as if in surrender. "Sorry. Some habits are hard to break."

She laughed, widening her stride to get across before the light turned again and barred their progress. "You take your cousin's elbow when you're guiding him through a crowd?"

"He's taller." She threw him a quizzical look as they reached the other side of the street. "I have a tendency to want to protect whoever's smaller than me." Which, he knew, included a large portion of the general population. If he'd worded it to say something about weaker than him or more vulnerable, he had a feeling he'd be in mortal peril. The corners of his mouth quirked in a smile. "It's the uniform that does it."

Walking up to the sandwich shop's glass

doors, she deliberately pulled one open, then held it for him. "I'll keep that in mind."

Collin merely shook his head tolerantly as he stepped inside.

The late afternoon sun had trouble pushing its way into the small, almost airless studio apartment with its black, sooty windows that faced the back of a tire factory. It could have been any season outside the small perimeter. Inside was a place where desperate people came with their hard-gotten money to buy new names. To trade their lives for someone else's in the hope that the new name would bring them more luck. Or at least enable them to escape the bad kind.

Word of mouth had brought Jason here. Word of mouth and the same kind of desperation that brought the others. Desperation fueled with hate because he had been temporarily reduced to this, to being as common as the others when he was so much better.

So much better than the man who sat in the filthy room, his ink-stained hand stretched out. Waiting.

Swallowing a loathsome curse, Jason doled out the bills from his wallet slowly. The cache of money he'd had the good sense to put by in case of an emergency was dwindling. It put him in a more foul mood than he was in already.

The ugly little man peering up at him from where he sat at the computer was demanding twice as much as they had originally agreed upon when he'd called to make the arrangements.

He hated being taken.

"That's my price." The man looked up at him, not flinching. Like a man who had crawled out of the jaws of death once and had nothing to lose anymore. "You want this passport," the reedy voice taunted Jason, "you come up with the money. Otherwise I toss it." He glanced down at the handiwork he'd just painstakingly created. "Makes no difference to me."

It would make a difference to the bastard if he shoved a blade between his ribs, Jason thought angrily. He'd already stabbed a prison guard. But he didn't have the knife anymore. About to pull it out of the second guard's chest, he thought he'd heard a car approaching the van. Hesitation would have had him risking his freedom and nothing was about to make him risk that. He'd fled from the scene like a hunted animal.

It was only after he'd reached the cover of trees that he realized his knife was still back in the van. Still in the wound where he'd left it.

But any knife would do in a pinch, he thought.

The kitchen sink was less than ten steps away. He could see a knife lying on the counter. There was a yellowish substance—mustard, margarine, something of that variety—encrusted on the blade, but that wouldn't matter. Dirty or not, it could still take a life if it was shoved in hard enough in the right place.

As to right places, his education in that department was certainly growing.

And the next time he left a man for dead, the man damn well would be, Jason fumed angrily, thinking of the guard who was still alive, who was, according to today's freaking newspaper headlines, still battling for his life.

None of this would have made the headlines if it hadn't somehow involved Ryan Fortune, he thought angrily. He even owed his notoriety to that bastard.

Jason could feel hatred filling his throat like bitter bile.

"There." He tossed the rest of the bills onto the desk in front of the man who had created his new passport for him. His ticket to freedom. Whenever he wished it.

The gnarled man at the desk made no reply. Instead he picked up the bills and counted them out, one by one. Satisfied as to their amount, he took out a hand-held light, slowly passed it over the bills one at a time, its bluish light glowing eerily over each.

Impatience all but strangled Jason. The document creator had the passport hostage beneath the last of the bills. He continued turning them over, one by one.

"What the hell are you doing?" Jason demanded hotly.

The smaller man's voice was as quiet, as calm, as Jason's was not. "Making sure you're not passing any counterfeit money to me." He cackled like an old warlock. "Can't be too careful these days."

"This is ridiculous," Jason railed. He reached for the passport, but the other man merely pulled it closer to him and continued reviewing the bills. Jason uttered a ripe curse. "If I could do that, you stupid fool, don't you think I could produce a passport without having to come to the likes of you?"

Eyes that seemed colorless in the poor light

raised from their task to look at him. The tolerance there galled Jason.

"True. Very true," the counterfeiter finally admitted, enjoying the humor he found in the ironic question. When he laughed again, Jason found the sound grating and irritating. Very carefully, the other man made a neat pile out of the money, then retrieved the passport from its place on the bottom.

He held it out to Jason. "Here you go, Mr. Jordan Pullman. A new passport to take you on a magic carpet ride anywhere in the world." He laughed again, tucking the money away.

The man was still laughing as Jason left. Jason slammed the door behind him, wanting to get as much distance between himself and the insane man in the airless apartment as possible.

He would have wanted to get as much distance as he could between himself and Red Rock, but there was still unfinished business left for him to tend to. There was the matter of the guard who still needed to be finally silenced.

And he wanted to see Ryan Fortune in his grave before he left for parts unknown. It was, after all, what had become the driving force of his life. To see the other life not just ruined, but ended. In the most torturous fashion possible.

That was the only way any of this would be worth it.

Chapter 7

The moment Collin and Lucy walked into the small sandwich shop, they were hit with a solid wall of humanity, all intent on eventually snaking their way past a short counter where five workers, all below the age of twenty-two, were furiously filling orders, their plastic-gloved hands flying almost as fast as the speed of sound.

Despite the crew's speed, it took fifteen minutes before they got their turn to order. After telling the young male with the shaven head what she wanted, Lucy looked at her watch.

Damn, it was later than she thought. No

time to sit, even if they could find a place to accommodate them both. "I'm going to have to get this to go."

Collin glanced at the kid behind the counter. Watching his hands, Collin couldn't help wondering how long it would take him to safely disassemble an automatic weapon.

Just the military in him, he supposed. He viewed most of life in khaki colors.

Catching the server's eye, he nodded toward Lucy. "You heard the lady."

Without missing a beat, the server reached for a sheet of waxed paper and neatly wrapped it around the sandwich. It was a mini-work of art.

"One ham and Swiss on sourdough with pickles, tomato, lettuce and green pepper plus diet soda to go." He had it bagged and on top of the counter in less time than it took to say it. Quoting a price, the server accepted the ten that Collin passed him.

As if it suddenly dawned on Lucy that there was only one sandwich going anywhere, she said. "You're not eating."

Collecting the change the server handed him, Collin tossed it into the almost-empty jar marked "Tips." Nobody realized how little these kids made, he thought. The change made a tinkling sound as it hit the side of the glass.

He took the bag and presented it to Lucy as he turned from the counter. "Not hungry."

"Haven't you heard, Lieutenant? An army travels on its stomach." They snaked their way out of the small shop, forging a path against the tide of incoming customers.

Normally he welcomed distance and anonymity, but the formality created by having her address him by his title bothered him. He wasn't sure exactly why and that bothered him, as well.

"I'm not in uniform. You don't have to call me Lieutenant."

She made her way to the corner before looking back at him and asking in a voice he found incredibly sultry, "What would you like me to call you?"

Something tightened in his gut, threatening to cut off his air. "Collin will be fine."

Lucy looked at him for a long moment as they stood there, waiting for the light to turn green. She had no idea what possessed her to say, "I'm sure Collin will be," only that it seemed right at the time.

Not only had his gut tightened some more, but now the sensation was working its way up his chest to his throat. He could have sworn something was stirring inside of him again. The way it did every time she raised those eyes of hers up to his.

The light turned green and she started to place one foot off the curb when he caught her by the arm and brought her attention back to him.

The cool air around them solidified. The people intent on getting on with their lives and doing it all in under an hour, melted into the background. Into just so much distant noise, along with the cars.

Under oath, Collin might have said he was momentarily possessed. Possessed by curiosity, possessed by a nostalgia that came flooding in from the past, a past that hadn't included her and yet did by virtue of a vague association, because she looked so much like Paula. Possessed by a hunger that he hadn't known for a very long time and because it had been so long ago, it was as if it had been someone else's hunger. Not his.

Until now.

Cupping her cheek, Collin brought his mouth down to hers and kissed her.

He surprised himself more than her, because something inside of her had been waiting for this.

Expecting this.

From the first second she'd seen him walk into the M.E.'s office, something had gone off in her head, a warning cry like the one uttered by that impossibly ridiculous robot in that equally impossibly ridiculous program that had been belovedly campy even in the year of its origin. *Danger, Lucy Gatling. Danger.*

The show popped up with a fair amount of regularity on cable and satellite stations that needed to fill their airwaves with programs they referred to as "classic." What she was feeling right at this moment, beyond overwhelmingly hot, could definitely be labeled as classic.

The sensation pulsating through her as he held her to him, deepening an already bottomless kiss, was as old as the ancient hills, as new and fresh as tomorrow.

Her heart pounded wildly while she leaned her body into his, and she forgot where she was, who she was. She forgot absolutely everything but the taste of his mouth and the excitement popping up in her veins like so many firecrackers going off at random.

"Hey, get a room!" someone in the distance heckled.

The words penetrated Collin, dragging with them common sense, reason and reality. It was a sobering sensation. He pulled back and stopped kissing her.

The moment he did, Lucy sucked in a long, deep breath, her eyes unwavering on his. It took a second for her to remember that English, not gibberish, was her first language.

"Yes," she murmured more to herself than to him, recalling the last thing she'd said to him before the world had gone completely out of focus. "Collin is certainly fine."

And then, as if realizing what she'd just said, she cleared her throat. The light was turning green again and Lucy stepped off the curb in a second attempt to reach his vehicle, not altogether sure if her legs were functioning properly. God knew she didn't feel as if she was functioning properly.

Reaching the car, she made it to the passenger side. But before getting in, she looked at him. She had to know. "Was that some kind of a test?"

She wasn't the only one trying to get her bearings. That had been completely out of character for Collin. Maybe if he'd been that way with Paula, he thought, she might still be with him. But Paula had never threatened his insides with utter meltdown the way this woman did.

Reminding himself that he was a Ranger and supposedly unflappable, he did his best to live up to that as he looked at her quizzically.

He hadn't the slightest idea what she was talking about. "What?"

"What just happened now, between us," she said, pointing to him and then herself. "Was that a test?"

He still didn't have a clue. "A test?" he echoed.

"Yes. Were you trying to see what I'd do next—kiss back," she responded without so much as a pause, "or if I could be rattled? I can, but not so most people would notice. Or—"

He held his hand up to stop her. No thought process at all had accompanied his kissing her. If he had to sum it up in a word, other than *possessed,* he would have used *desire,* because that had throbbed through him as urgently as a rising tide pounding against the shore.

"Maybe," he suggested, "I was just trying to earn a little peace and quiet."

Those would have been the last words she

would have used to describe what was going on inside of her at this very moment.

Opening the car door as Collin unlocked the vehicle, she slanted a glance at him. "Back-fired on you, didn't it, Lieutenant?"

He saw no reason for pretense—up to a point. "Certainly did."

Lucy smiled warmly at him as they got into the car. "I guess that's what's known as a sneak attack."

No, he thought, that was better described as a blitzkrieg. "Sneak attacks are a lot more subtle than that."

Her smile widened, taking in her eyes as he watched in fascination. "I'll remember to be on my guard."

Collin glanced at his watch. He was run-ning late himself. But then, he hadn't factored in time for the dalliance. "And for now, I'd better be on my mark," he told her. She gave him a curious look. "My cousin's meeting us at the M.E.'s."

That made, what? Three times in one day? "You know, you boys are going to have to get a new hangout. The chief medical exam-iner doesn't like people just dropping in, un-announced. Not unless they have their clothes off and are lying on a gurney." Collin grinned at her and she could feel the beginning of another blush. She would have sworn she was past all that, and yet here he was, doing it to her twice in a single day. "You know what I mean."

"I do." Buckling up, he was about to start the car and glanced to see if she'd put her seat belt in place. "Where's your sandwich?"

Stunned, Lucy looked down at her lap as if expecting it to magically appear there.

And then she remembered. "You made me drop it." Craning her neck, she tried to scan the area around the traffic light. But there were too many people in the way for her to see if the bag was still there on the ground.

Most likely not. With a sigh, she sat back.

She heard him laugh under his breath. "Never had that effect on a woman before."

Her stomach growled and she tried to ignore it. Lucy had no idea whether or not he was pulling her leg. She had a feeling that Lieutenant Collin Jamison made women drop more than just their sandwiches when he put his mind to it.

Lucy chewed on her bottom lip, staring at the report spread out in front of her on the small steel-topped desk that had been assigned to her for the duration of her stay at the M.E.'s office. The notes had yet to be entered into a database and were written in what could only be charitably likened to a hog's hooves dipped in black ink and allowed to run amock.

But illegible or not, she'd pored over it and was finally rewarded for her efforts.

She had something.

Not a big something and certainly not the DNA confirmation that Collin was looking for, but she had a brand-new piece to add to the puzzle that was Jason Jamison's case. Flipping through the man's file, she'd stumbled across an incident report filed by the guard on duty while Jason was in prison. It seemed that Collin's cousin'd had a "difference of opinion" with another one of the inmates. The latter had wound up in the infirmary with his face almost bashed in. Jason had one hell of a temper.

She read further, looking at the guard's signature. Her eyes widened.

Her first impulse was to find Harley and tell him. As the M.E. assigned to instruct her, he needed to be informed about this. But then she hesitated. She'd told Collin that she'd let him know if she found anything unusual.

This certainly came under that heading.

She chewed a little more on her lip, then

made her decision. Closing the file, she placed it beneath several others, then walked out of the sterile room and into the hall.

Lucy dug through the oversize pockets of her lab coat, looking for the cell phone number Collin had given her. Finding it, she put some distance between herself and the autopsy room, then took out a red, white and blue cell phone her father had given her the last time they'd gotten together. It operated under her old number, but he thought that the colors would remind her of her family.

As if she needed some kind of gimmick to keep them foremost in her mind, she thought.

Looking at the card, Lucy quickly pressed the matching buttons on the keypad and waited until the call registered on the other end.

It only rang once before she heard someone say, "Hello?"

The deep male voice against her ear sent ripples clear down to her stomach. Evoking visions of yesterday. Reminding her that she'd spent a rather restless night, tossing and turning as she tried not to think about what had happened on the street corner.

Lucy unconsciously squared her shoulders before she spoke. As if a military stance would somehow protect her. "Lieutenant?"

"Doctor," Collin responded formally, employing a teasing tone.

With absolutely no effort at all, she could have easily allowed her thoughts to drift back to yesterday afternoon. But that had already taken up most of her night. If she allowed that same teeth-jarring moment to get a toehold in her day, she knew she would be rendered useless. That had pretty much been her entire evening as it dribbled into morning.

She was in serious need of a brain transplant, she told herself.

"I think I just might have found another piece of the puzzle for you."

There was silence on the other end. She was beginning to know the lieutenant a little. He was trying not to get his hopes up. What would Collin have been like, hopeful? She decided that she wanted to be the one to bring hope to him, for the sheer pleasure of witnessing his reaction.

"What is it?"

Lucy could almost see Collin straightening his shoulders, which were already ramrod-straight.

"The day before Jason was to be transferred to the maximum security prison, he got into a fight with another inmate." She kept her voice low, afraid of being overheard. "Beat him up pretty badly before it was stopped. The guy had to have a total of forty stitches in three different places."

She heard Collin snort. "The guy packs quite a wallop."

Lucy paused for effect, then delivered the crowning touch. "There's more."

"I'm listening."

"One of the guards on duty during this initial altercation, the one who actually signed the report, was the transport guard who's currently fighting for his life at the hospital."

"Interesting."

She could see him stroking his chin thoughtfully, pulling together scenarios in his head. "It's more than interesting. That means that there's a connection between them. It's possible that the guard might have even hid the knife for Jason."

He could feel her excitement vibrating through the cell phone. He had to admit that it fueled his own. In a number of ways. "Yeah, like on the van. He could have been the inside man."

But if that were true, then she'd hit a stumbling block. "Then why stab him, too?"

She was assigning her own sensibilities to

Jason, Collin thought. Her own moral code. He knew better than to do that. The heart that beat within Jason's chest was nothing more than pure lead.

"Jason never liked leaving behind any loose ends. He was always very meticulous as a kid. The guard represents a loose end. Maybe," he theorized, trying to rein in his own growing excitement over this newest piece of evidence, "he even knows or overheard where Jason planned on going once he escaped from prison."

"According to what you told me, that's not going to be immediately. Not if he's got some kind of a vendetta against Ryan Fortune. If he does, then he's got to be around here somewhere, waiting for his chance to get at Mr. Fortune." She heard him laugh on the other end. The sound was warm, enticing. She had to struggle not to let herself be pulled in by it. "What's so funny?"

"You know, if I was the kind of man who could be spooked, I think that I'd be pretty spooked right about now."

She didn't follow him. "Why?"

"Because we think alike. I didn't think anyone thought the way I did." Least of all, a woman.

The only one who had come close to it had been Paula and even she had only gone so far. As time progressed, because of his work, he had to admit that they had gotten farther and farther apart. What he missed, he realized, was the idea of Paula. The idea of comfort and status quo without effort.

But effort was what this woman seemed to be all about. And he rather liked it.

"Right back at you," she quipped. She'd been rather surprised herself on how they'd arrived at the same conclusion regarding the information she'd uncovered.

"Anything else?" he prodded when she said nothing further.

"What, that isn't enough for you?" Just what did the man want? A call from her saying that Jason was presently hiding out in her house?

"More than enough," he assured her. "You've just earned yourself one lavish dinner."

She cleared her throat, as if making a bid for his attention. "I'm still waiting for the lunch you zapped me out of."

"That wasn't my fault."

That wasn't the way she saw it. "As far as I remember, I don't recall anyone else's lips being on mine at the time."

He laughed, but the next question out of his mouth was a serious one. "Have you told anyone else about the connection you found?"

Guilt shimmied up and down her spine as she thought of Harley. She didn't want to get the physician into trouble with the chief medical examiner by failing to tell him about the report. And yet, her loyalties did lie with Collin. At least for the moment.

"Not yet."

"Good. Hold off for a little while," he requested. "First let me get in contact with Emmett and tell him about this."

"Don't wait too long to get back to me." She realized how that must have sounded to him. "I mean, I'll need to write this up eventually. They're having me do a little background work—for practice, I suppose."

"Well, you've gone from practice to perfect," he told her. "I'll get back to you," he repeated.

The line went dead in her hand before she could say anything in response.

Perfect.

That was the word he'd used. Perfect.

It shimmered in her mind like some sort of rare enticement. For a basically simple man, the lieutenant knew how to use his words to their best advantage. And his.

With a sigh, Lucy folded her phone and slipped it back into her pocket. When she turned to head back to the lab, she saw that Harley was standing only a few feet away, watching her, a reproving expression on his face.

Refusing to allow guilt to get the better of her, Lucy offered him the sunniest smile she had at her disposal as she walked past him and went back into the morgue. The room seemed like a haven to her now.

She realized that she was becoming accustomed to the eeriness there and began to wonder if that was such a good thing.

She waited for Harley to enter and begin asking vague, unfocused questions to get to his point, but the door leading into the room remained closed. After a few moments she decided he wasn't coming.

With a sigh of relief she got back to work. There were other reports waiting for her besides the one she'd turned into her own personal crusade because of a man with a sexy smile and killer eyes.

Chapter 8

It took Lucy a moment to realize that she was no longer alone in the room.

So deeply immersed in reading over the reports of past autopsies plus the notes pertaining to the police investigations attached to them to get a feel for what exactly might tip the scales of justice, she hadn't heard the door to the morgue being opened.

Nor did she hear anyone walk in.

But even as she looked up, she knew that whoever had entered wasn't Harley or any of the other doctors associated with the medical examiner's office. The others made noise as they walked in.

The man who had entered was accustomed to moving around like a shadow. Without a sound.

Though she tried her best to stifle her reaction, she'd started when she saw him. It was like seeing someone walk out of her dreams and into her afternoon.

Taking off her glasses, Lucy rubbed the bridge of her nose, buying herself some time and trying to put on a composed face. Wearing glasses gave her a headache, but if she wanted to be able to read the fine print that was sometimes included in the notes, it was a necessary evil.

Lucy looked at her invader. He was wearing jeans again, along with his leather jacket. The imported leather was probably the softest thing about him, she mused. "Do you always sneak up on people?"

"I wasn't sneaking," he told her. "I was being quiet." And then, because being around her made him feel relaxed and alert all at the same time, Collin allowed himself a smile. "I suppose it's what you call an occu-pational habit."

Lucy put her glasses down on the desk on top of the files she hadn't gotten to yet. Questions rose in her mind. They seemed to pop up in her head every time she saw him. This, she knew, she had no business asking, but she couldn't help herself.

"How dangerous is the life you lead?"

The question caught him off guard. He wasn't here to discuss hazards of the field. He was here because she could help. Because he paid his debts, no matter how small. And because he liked looking at her. "It all depends on whom I'm facing."

She found herself smiling and told herself she was being adolescent. But seeing as how she'd never really gone through that stage in its entirety the first time around, she supposed she could be forgiven a little back-sliding every now and then.

"Usually," she elaborated.

Collin shrugged carelessly as he parked one hip against the steel desk. "No more than the average soldier."

Average her foot. No one associated with Special Ops was anywhere near "average." "Who's been parachuted behind enemy lines," she completed.

So, she was a romantic, as well. Interesting combination, he thought.

"Never parachuted," he corrected quietly.

"That's giving the enemy much too big a target."

He'd been dropped off on coastlines, crawled across borders into enemy terrain, always in the dead of a moonless night. There was also a host of other ways of slipping in behind enemy lines that were more intricate and more stealthy, which meant that, ultimately, they were safer.

For about a minute and a half.

He never let his guard down for that long.

He wasn't about to now, with her.

Lucy might not be the enemy, but that didn't mean she wasn't a threat to life as he knew it.

She leaned back in her chair, deliberately pushing it away from the desk. Having Collin so close at this angle, smelling of some aftershave that caused her to want to have been there way before he began shaving this morning, overwhelmed her. She didn't like being at a disadvantage, even around someone as seemingly honorable as Collin.

Especially around someone like Collin, she amended silently. There wasn't just danger in his eyes; it was there in every move he made. It had certainly been in his kiss. In her heart, she knew a woman would do well to be watchful around him.

She craned her neck, looking behind him. "Where's your cousin?"

He and Emmett had talked it over and decided they might be able to cover more ground if they split up.

"Out doing what he does best. Wearing people down." He saw her eyebrows rise in a silent query. "Emmett's trying his hand at attempting to get into the investigation through normal channels. The FBI frowns on family connections in investigations," he added, but he had a hunch she already knew that.

Collin doubted, young though this woman looked, that there was very much Lucy Gatling wasn't up on or that managed to escape her. That was part of what attracted him to her.

He didn't allow himself to dwell, even fleetingly, on her other compelling parts. It wouldn't be productive.

"If he's busy doing that, what are you doing here? Come to pick my brain some more?" She shook her head, indicating that he'd miscalculated. "I don't have anything new to offer you."

He didn't know about that. From where he was standing, the woman had a great deal to offer him, new or otherwise. But he wasn't here about that, he told himself firmly, then relented slightly because that wasn't altogether true. At least some of the reason why he was here had to do with her. Not with what she could do for him, but with *her.*

"I owe you two meals," he told her casually. "I thought that maybe it was time to start paying up." He glanced at his watch. "Isn't it about your lunchtime?" He knew it was. He'd already looked into that to make certain it was.

She'd brought an orange and a sandwich with her in a paper sack. "Are you sure you have time for it? You don't have to do this, you know."

Lucy didn't want him here out of some sense of obligation. A sense of obligation could be a daunting, dehumanizing emotion at times. It was what had forced Jeff to marry that woman who was carrying his baby. The woman he didn't love. In her heart, she'd always felt that, given enough time, Jeff would have returned her love. If he hadn't allowed himself to be swayed by one night of passion, which ultimately resulted in a lifetime commitment he wasn't ready for.

Collin's eyes locked with hers. "Sure I do. Are you ready?"

The last question seemed to undulate along her skin, causing her mind to scramble. All she could think of in response was that she had been born ready for him.

That wasn't the right answer, she told herself. She cleared her throat.

"Excuse me?" she asked.

The almost wicked smile that took possession of his lips didn't help her mental state settle down.

"For lunch," Collin explained. "Are you ready for lunch?"

Seeing as how her pulse was suddenly determined to institute a new rhythm, maybe going out to lunch with him wasn't the wisest thing to agree to right now. She pretended to glance at the work she had yet to do, silently using it as an excuse. "You really don't have to," she repeated.

She was resisting, but Collin got the feeling that she truly didn't want to resist. That made two of them. Because he wanted to share a little time with this woman. Share it in some nice, well-trafficked place where he wasn't tempted to do anything stupid.

Yeah, right, he mocked himself, like the way a crowd had prevented him from doing yesterday.

"Yes, I do have to," he informed her, his eyes never leaving hers. "A man's only as good as his word, and I said I'd buy you lunch—and dinner."

She gave him a way out. "Technically, you already bought me lunch."

He grinned and she felt her insides unraveling at a faster clip. "Yes, but as I recall, I'm also to blame for you leaving it behind."

She inclined her head, feeling both embarrassed and excited at the same time. She searched for a response. "Not often I'm thrown a curve like that."

Yes, he supposed that was one way to look at it. For both of them. "I don't usually throw a curve like that."

For the first time since she'd met him, she glanced at his hand, looking for a wedding ring, something she realized she hadn't checked for before. It would be just her luck to get emotionally involved with a man who was already spoken for.

There was no ring, no tan line for one, but that didn't mean anything. Her father had never worn a wedding ring, either.

Self-preservation kicked in. She took the offensive. "Are you married, Lieutenant?"

"Man in my line of work doesn't get married."

Well, that was certainly putting her on notice, Lucy thought. He had no intentions of making this serious. But it was good to know, because that meant she wouldn't be in danger of accidentally trying to raise this to a higher plateau.

Knowing it couldn't go anywhere freed her from concerns that she might make a misstep that would take her to a place where her principles might have to battle it out with her emotions. Simply put, she meant to stay pure until she married. But she was smart enough to know that her emotions might not see it that way. Especially since this lieutenant was causing them to scramble.

She decided to continue to feel him out. "I see. Married to your work?"

"Let's just say I'm never in one place long enough to make that kind of a commitment." Talking about his private life, of what went on inside his head, always made him feel restless. He needed to move on to another, safer subject. "So, you never answered my question. Are you ready?"

He wasn't going to take no for an answer. She could see him as an operative, taking that same stand. Except with a deadlier glint to it.

The image sent a little thrill through her that she squelched a beat too late.

Lucy forced herself to focus on his question. They were pretty lax when it came to hours at the medical examiner's. As long as she did the work expected of her, there was leeway.

Lucy rose from the chair, pushing it back against the desk. "Yes."

Straightening, Collin moved away from the desk. "What are you in the mood for?"

A repeat performance of yesterday by the crosswalk, please.

She pressed her lips together, pretending to think. Hoping that no pink color had leached out onto her skin again. She took her three-quarter coat out of the locker where it was housed. "I've had food from all four corners of the world. Surprise me."

He frowned, unprepared for her answer. Taking the coat from her, he helped her on with it. "I'm not good at surprises."

She sincerely doubted that. Turning around, she pulled her hair out from beneath the coat. She had a hunch that he was very, very good at surprises. Both in the field and off.

Still, Lucy decided to play along. "All right, I'll make it easy. Mexican. As a matter of fact, I know just the place."

He let her take the lead.

* * *

The restaurant belonging to Jose and Maria Mendoza, simply called Red, was extremely popular. It was also very crowded at this time of day. But luck was with them and they managed to find the last available table on the premises, securing it a beat before another couple.

Collin slipped out of his jacket, letting it fall over the back of his chair as he watched the woman he'd brought. She looked like a soft little thing, but there was a strength there beneath the softness.

Just as there had been in her kiss.

He took a long drink of the water at the table.

The waitress, a pretty dark-haired girl with even darker eyes, came to their table almost immediately. "May I bring you something to drink?" she asked in a lyrical voice that held just a hint of a Mexican accent in it.

Since he found himself not exactly thinking clearly, he ordered a margarita rather than his usual bourbon, neat.

"And for the lady?"

Thinking of the long afternoon ahead of her, Lucy was about to demur, then decided that one drink would be all right. After all, it wasn't as if she couldn't hold her liquor. In her late teens she'd discovered that she had a great tolerance for alcohol. Something else that being with Jeff had taught her, along with the lesson that had left an indelible mark on her soul: giving your heart away could get you in trouble. And bring with it a boatload of disappointment.

The boat had docked in her harbor, never allowing her to forget what she'd learned. It had been almost ten years now, but it was just as fresh in her mind today as it was when it had first happened. When she'd fallen in love with Jeff only to lose him to someone who was far more aggressive, far more into "the game," even when that so-called game took on very serious stakes.

"I didn't picture you as someone who enjoyed a drink," he commented when the drinks arrived.

She took a sip of the beverage. "I don't pigeonhole well, Lieutenant."

He raised his glass in a silent toast to her. "Obviously."

Along with the drinks, they'd ordered a plate of nachos with its accompanying special cheese sauce as an appetizer. In the background, the mellow sounds of a solo guitarist making love to his guitar came slowly drifting to their table.

For the duration of the meal, though she knew she shouldn't, Lucy pretended that there was no clock ticking the minutes away.

When the main course arrived, the servings turned out to be huge.

"They certainly believe in giving you your money's worth," he commented as he watched the waitress set the plate down in front of him.

The woman flashed him an inviting smile before withdrawing. It was not lost on Lucy. It reminded her that she and Collin came from two different worlds. His being the one with an abundance of experience, among other things.

She lowered her eyes to her enchilada, pretending to give it her undivided attention. "You are hereby officially absolved of any debt you feel you owe me," she told him. "This covers lunch *and* dinner."

He paused to read between the lines. And discovered that the lines were a little blurred. "Listening to you, someone would get the impression that you don't like my company."

She looked up. Then someone would be very, very wrong, she thought.

Because he was looking at her so intently,

she shrugged. "It's not that. I don't like being in debt to someone and I imagine neither do you."

He didn't view this as a debt in the true sense of the word. Not when he was enjoying himself. He'd come to a point in his life where he thought he'd forgotten how. But he hadn't. And she had brought it out of him. "Not unless that debt has compensations."

Afraid that he might be using her, she jumped to the most logical conclusion. "Like DNA information?"

He didn't bother denying the obvious. They *did* need confirmation. But that wasn't all of it. "Among other things."

His words, his tone, hung in the air between them. "I don't follow." She raised her eyes to his.

And then she did follow.

Her breath caught in her throat.

But maybe, she warned herself tersely, she was reading too much into this. Maybe, she insisted, Military Man was just being friendly because she had access to things that he couldn't get at through regular channels, short of breaking into the M.E.'s office.

Not that she didn't think he could. She could envision him making locks do his bidding, stealthily making his way through the dark and bypassing security alarms with ease to get what he wanted.

But it was probably much easier and less complicated wining and dining a third-year medical student, she thought ruefully.

Collin could see by the look in her eyes that they understood each other—and that she was overthinking things, as well.

Maybe it was better that way. If she was leery of him, it just might keep him from making a mistake, the way he had yesterday. Although while it was happening it certainly hadn't *felt* like a mistake. Kissing her had given him an incredible rush that seemed endless. It contained more kick to it than the drink he was now nursing.

Just remembering the moment made him want to lean over the small table for two to see if her lips had the same potency today as they had yesterday. Or if yesterday had happened because he was still chasing a dream and living with regret.

The look in his eyes made Lucy warm. She knew it had nothing to do with the drink in her hand. Desperate to find a neutral subject, something that wouldn't send her thoughts running to places where they didn't belong, she asked suddenly, "Are you going to need any help?"

He looked down at his plate, wondering if she was inordinately hungry. "I think I can manage."

"No," Lucy laughed, "I meant with the investigation. You said something about wanting to talk with Jason's former neighbors and co-workers." One slim shoulder lifted in a disparaging way, then fell again. "Maybe I could help."

A small furrow formed between his eyes. "Aren't you busy with your work?"

She was the kind of person for whom multitasking was a religion. She could step up her pace, finishing faster and applying herself to something else.

"Yes, but I'm thinking that Jason's neighbors might be working until five, six o'clock. They won't be coming home until the early evening. We could go then. I'd be someone more reachable to talk to. After all, I'm with the M.E.'s office. People find the medical examiner's officer a lot less intimidating than the FBI or the CIA. You people need a better publicist."

She flashed him a quirky smile. As she spoke, she fingered the badge that hung from the chord around her neck, tying that in to what she'd just said.

Collin could just see it. A newer, *friendlier* CIA. It wouldn't fly with the powers that be. And an agency that was less intimidating might not have accomplished as much as it had now.

"You might get into trouble," he cautioned her.

"I wouldn't tell them I was there officially. Just that I'm with the M.E.'s office. Which is true. I am. Until they rotate me out."

A certain admiration came into his eyes. "You're not new to lying, are you?"

"I had two strict parents who weren't sure how to go about the job of parenting a teenage daughter who'd tasted her share of freedom. Besides, it's not lying, it's all in how you arrange the words. It's not my fault if people happen to understand one thing when I meant something else entirely."

He rolled her suggestion over in his head. "You know, I think you might be helpful at that."

While he was good at reading people, at picking up signs, at least on an impersonal level, he wasn't always good when it came to saying the right thing to get them talking.

He supposed that was where his interpersonal skills could use a little upgrading. "What time do you get off?"

"Five. Used to be six, but I think they feel there's only so many hours a med student should be subjected to dead people."

If he were to guess what she did, working in the medical examiner's office and performing autopsies would have been the last thing he would have selected. "I could see how that might get daunting. How does someone like you put up with it?"

"The same way a person like you does," she told him sweetly.

An alarm went off. He'd treaded on her toes, he thought. She took her work, her place in the scheme of things, seriously. He could easily relate to that.

"Sorry, no disrespect intended. It's just that you're so young."

What was she, Lucy thought, a handful of years younger than he was? She didn't want him thinking of her as some adolescent barely out of her teens.

"Nobody who has been told her mother died 'in the line of duty' is young."

Died in the line of duty. How familiar he was with that line. The military's standard issue. It covered a whole myriad of incidents, from the obvious to the covert. He looked at her with interest. Had her mother been an operative?

Curiosity nudged at him with more force than he was accustomed to. "I'm sorry. I didn't know."

She smiled. "Because I didn't tell you."

"Is that all you know?" he prodded as he finished his serving. "That your mother died in the line of duty?"

She could tell by the way he said it that he found the line suspect. Or at least worthy of exploration.

Lucy nodded, suppressing a sigh that had been with her ever since she'd been informed of her mother's death. "That's all they told my father." She debated for a second, then decided to share something with him she hadn't told anyone else. She wasn't altogether sure why. "I don't think he was ever privy to the full extent of what my mother did." She thought back to conversations she'd had with him, both before and after her death. "He was proud of her, I know that, but I think it got to him at times. There were questions he couldn't ask. Answers she couldn't give him. She'd look at him with that patient way of hers and say, 'John, you know I can't talk about that.'"

Lucy shook her head. That wasn't the way it was supposed to be. That wasn't the way it was going to be for her once she finally got married. "Husbands and wives shouldn't have secrets from each other. Even if the government is involved."

Which is exactly why I never intend to get married, Collin said to himself. It wouldn't be fair to either his wife or to him. And the strain of keeping his two lives separate would eventually tell on the marriage and break it apart. "What was your mother's name?"

She looked at him curiously. "Margaret," she said slowly. "Margaret Hannigan Gatling."

He nodded at the information, the wheels in his head already spinning. He thought he knew whom to check with. "Can't be too many of those around."

She didn't understand. Where was he going with this? "Why do you ask?"

"Maybe I can nose around a little, find some things out for you." He saw the light come into her eyes. "Return the favor."

She'd wanted to know for almost ten years now what had ended her mother's life. Specifically. "You could do that?"

Collin had never been one to make promises he wasn't a hundred percent sure he could keep. "I could try."

That was good enough for her. Lucy had a feeling that when Collin Jamison tried, he usually succeeded.

The smile that came to her lips arrived there through no effort at all.

Chapter 9

Collin flipped his cell phone closed just before he walked into the hotel restaurant. He was meeting Emmett for breakfast and to play a little catch-up.

The investigation was not going all that well. The feeling in his gut that Jason was somewhere around rather than heading out for parts unknown was still very much there.

He was going to need more time.

To that end, he'd put in a call to his C.O., talking to the colonel personally rather than going through his assistant. He asked for another week of R&R. He knew that Colonel Eagleton was too sharp a man to be fooled by the reason for the request. The last time Collin had an extended period of rest and relaxation, he'd broken his leg while skiing during Christmas vacation, and had to stay off his feet for the longest two weeks of his life. He'd been thirteen at the time.

Fortunately, Colonel Eagleton was sharp enough not to ask questions of a man who gave a hundred and ten percent of himself when he was on the job. Which was almost always.

Wrapping his hand around the doorknob, Collin sighed just before walking through the double glass doors that led into the cheery restaurant located on the ground floor of his hotel. It'd been a week since he'd undertaken this, and still nothing.

Well, not nothing, he amended, his mouth curving almost involuntarily. Spotting Emmett at the table, he nodded and made his way over.

He had been spending a lot of time with Lucy. More time, actually, than he had been with Emmett, a fact that hadn't been lost on his cousin, even though the latter seemed totally oblivious to anything beyond his crusade to bring Jason back in.

As Collin pulled out the chair for himself, the waitress appeared, a carafe in her hand.

"Coffee?"

She looked at him as if she couldn't imagine anyone saying no to the dark brew at this hour of the morning.

Collin slid into the chair. "Please."

Once she'd filled the cup, he gave his order without bothering to look at the menu. They had eaten here every morning since his arrival. There was no reason to suspect that anything new had been added to the plastic-coated sheet.

The waitress retreated, leaving a sunny smile in her wake.

"So, how's it going between you and the M.E.-in-training?" Emmett asked, coming out of his self-imposed silence.

Collin looked at him in surprise. During the day their paths had taken them in separate directions. He'd mentioned Lucy to Emmett in passing once or twice. He'd expected the whole of their conversation this morning to be about the most recent leads to Jason's whereabouts, not anything this personal.

He raised the cup to his lips and took a sip of the hot brew. Whoever made the coffee this morning had outdone themselves, he thought. His whole system seemed to come awake with a jolt.

"She's planning on working in forensics, not the medical examiner's office," he corrected his cousin absently. He didn't even have to look to know that Emmett's eyes were still on him. "What?"

The vague shrug gave nothing away. Neither did Emmett's expression.

"Nothing. Just can't remember you ever being caught up with a woman before." He paused significantly, then added, "Not since Paula."

The waitress had returned. He waited for her to leave the plate of three small pancakes, decorated with a piece of bacon on top, before replying.

When he did, there was a slight frown on his lips. "She's nothing like Paula, if that's where you're going."

The look on Emmett's face told Collin that he wasn't as convinced. "Same coloring, same bone structure."

Collin snorted, dismissing the analogy. "A mountain lion's in the same general family as a house cat. Doesn't make them alike."

Intrigued, needing to be diverted if only for a moment, Emmett cocked his head. "And which is the fledgling doctor—the mountain lion or the house cat?"

"Doesn't matter."

Emmett continued to look at him as he ate. With an impatient shrug, Collin said, "Mountain lion."

Emmett put his own interpretation to the answer. "You saying she's dangerous?"

That hadn't occurred to Collin. In his mind's eye, he could see Lucy, the way her hands and whole body seemed to join in whatever she was saying. The woman was nothing if not animated.

"No. Vibrant. Alive."

Emmett nodded to himself. "Always a good thing in a girlfriend."

The fork slid from Collin's fingers. "Whoa, hold on there. How the hell did you make that jump?"

To which Emmett merely smiled. It was the kind of smile a cat might have upon discovering that the white liquid in its dish wasn't milk but cream. "You're not the only one who notices things."

Collin snorted again, this time with feeling. "Well, if that's how good you are, I'd say being up there alone in that mountain cabin has put you way off your game, cousin. There's nothing between Lucy and me." Emmett laughed.

The solitary sound was so rare, it brought Collin up short. "Now what?"

Emmett could only shake his head at his cousin. "You know, for an intelligent man, you can be very dumb sometimes."

Collin's eyes narrowed slightly. He'd never reacted well to being analyzed, even by someone he felt close to. "Meaning what?"

Emmett's expression told Collin that he was surprised he even had to ask. "Meaning that even a blind man could see that there are sparks between the two of you."

Collin casually picked up his cup and finished his coffee. The waitress appeared almost immediately to refill it.

He nodded his thanks, then looked at his cousin. "With you being the man, I'd say that description's just about right. Blind." He let the word sink in. "She's twenty-six." Lucy had confided that to him yesterday. He remembered thinking that seemed so young to him. "That's just starting out in life, Emmett. I'm too worn out for her."

"Collin, you're only thirty-five. For most men, that's their prime."

Sinking his fork into the pancake stack for another helping, Collin shrugged off his cousin's assessment. It wasn't about numbers, it was about feelings.

"I've been around too long in this game, seen too much. It changes a man, Emmett. You of all people should know that. Seeing what we have, it just siphons off hope about humanity."

That was part of what had sent him seeking a solitary life, Emmett thought. But he'd learned that life wasn't something you ran from. It had a habit of coming and finding you.

Besides, he didn't want to see Collin ending up like him—even though he was the younger of the two.

He drained his own cup, setting it down. Their waitress was busy with two new customers so there was no need to wait before delivering his assessment. "Then I'd say a dose of fresh, vibrant innocence is just what you need."

Collin laughed shortly. "You make her sound like a tonic."

Emmett appeared to roll that around in his head before answering. "Maybe she could be." A vague hint of a smile appeared. "A cure for what ails you."

Their eyes met. Collin gave him a meaningful look. "Look to your own house, Emmett."

Emmett allowed a sigh to escape. If only he could. This pursuit was stalled and it was making him very antsy. "That's what I'm trying to do."

"I didn't mean about Jason—" Just then, his cell phone went off. The opening notes of the "Battle Hymn of the Republic" drifted between them. Collin held his hand up to Emmett, indicating that they weren't through with their conversation. Flipping the cell phone open, he held it against his ear. "Jamison."

"Collin, the results from both DNA tests just came in."

He didn't have to ask. It was Lucy. Even if she hadn't mentioned the DNA tests, he recognized her voice even though she was whispering. The low and almost breathy voice undulated through his system. Making him alert. Making him very aware of all the responses that were simultaneously going on.

It took him a second to realize that she had called him Collin rather than referred to him by his rank. Had her excitement taken the formality out of their relationship? Or was her guard down and his name just tumbled from her lips?

He reminded himself that he wasn't here to wonder about nuances and things like cause and effect when they pertained to anything other than finding Jason and bringing him in.

Lucy, he mouthed to Emmett who'd raised a quizzical brow in his direction the moment he'd answered the cell phone.

"Speak of the devil," Emmett murmured just before he wiped his mouth with his napkin.

Collin tried to ignore his cousin. Ignore, too, that there was a part of him that wished Emmett was right about his view of Lucy. But it was all in his cousin's head. Vibrancy was just Lucy's way. It didn't have anything to do with him. The fact that he felt something, well, that wasn't to be explored here, either. One thing at a time was the way he got things done.

"Go ahead," he urged Lucy. "Did you find out anything?"

She gave him the negative news first. "The skin under the dead man's nails doesn't match your cousin's DNA at all."

He was aware that she hadn't lumped both tests together. That meant the other test had been positive. He just needed her to say it.

"And?" he prodded.

"And as for the second sample—" he could hear the smile in her voice, could almost see it on her face "—it's a hundred percent positive."

He began moving the puzzle piece around in his head, looking for somewhere to fit it to its best advantage. "Then the dead man did scratch the other guard."

"Appears that way."

"Fantastic." And then he paused, organizing his thoughts. "I guess you'd better give the results to the local police."

"Nope."

That was deliberately withholding evidence rather than just stalling for a few hours. He couldn't allow her to get into trouble on his account. He'd feel too responsible. "Lucy, you have to—"

She interrupted him. "They've been shut down. This case is now in the hands of the FBI. I can hold off for a few hours, say I got bogged down in paperwork and didn't get a chance to look at the results until, oh, say noon. So you want me to do that? Will that buy you anything significant?"

He paused. Neither he nor Emmett were after the glory of the case. They didn't want the "kill" personally. All either of them cared about was bringing Jason to justice any way possible. For killing Christopher. And to keep him from killing Ryan.

"No," he told her firmly. "Don't jeopardize yourself any more than you already have."

He heard the short intake of breath on the other end. Obviously he'd managed to tick her off. "I can take care of myself."

"I know you can." He could feel Emmett watching him, listening to his half of the conversation. Collin shifted restlessly. "But you're not going to wind up with a black mark on your records because of me."

The fact that he was being protective of her both made Lucy bristle and warmed her at the same time. She wished she'd had some kind of practice at this relationship thing. It was way too complex for her liking, scrambled too many things inside of her for that matter.

"Too late for that," she told him. "Once I bring this to the FBI's attention, they're going to want to know where I got the DNA samples to run against the blood and skin that were found under the dead driver's nails."

"You could say that I brought them to you. That you thought I was one of the people assigned to the case. Takes the blame off you."

And puts it squarely on you, she thought. "I'll handle it," she told him again, firmly this time, then paused for a moment. She hesitated, then pushed straight ahead. "Are we still on for later? I've got half a day coming to me."

He'd been meaning to get back to where the prison van had gone off the side of the road to check out the area. But it wasn't exactly an excursion for a woman.

Still, he knew if he mentioned that, she would definitely get her back up. "All right, I'll be by around noon."

She made a quick decision. "Good, that'll give me enough time to bring this to Harley's attention. He can bring it to the chief M.E. and it can go to the FBI from there. See you later."

The connection went dead before he could respond. He folded the phone and returned it to his pocket.

"Well?" Emmett prodded.

Collin shifted in his chair to face his cousin again. "The DNA under our dead man's nails matches the DNA from the second guard."

"Who's still locked away in some netherworld." According to the reports, the man hadn't regained consciousness even for a few moments. Emmett shook his head. "I keep thinking he might be the key to finding Jason. God knows nothing else is turning up any real leads." He blew out a breath, trying not to let impatience get to him. "Just ones that lead nowhere."

Between the two of them, they had re-interviewed a host of people both from Jason's former neighborhood and his place of work. No one who worked for Jason had had anything good to say about him. The man they'd known as Jason Wilkes had been driven and drove those around him relentlessly, feeling that what they did reflected on him. Nobody liked him. It was only to his superiors that he had shown a face devoid of a scowl.

As for his neighbors, none of the people who lived around him on the block could remember his ever having struck up a conversation with them. Two or three remembered seeing him going somewhere with his wife, or the woman they'd all thought was his wife. There hadn't been anything out of the ordinary there, either, except that everyone said that Melissa Wilkes had been a woman people noticed even in passing. Bright, vivacious, with an incredible figure, she dressed provocatively enough to make a dead man take notice.

Right now she was the most voluptuous woman in the cemetery, Collin thought darkly.

He realized that Emmett was rising from the table. Digging into his pocket, his cousin tossed a ten down on the table beside his cup. He slipped his wallet back into his pocket. "That should cover it."

The prices here were more than reasonable, even for a hotel restaurant. "You just had coffee," Collin pointed out.

"So?" A half smile graced his lips. "The rest can be a tip." He glanced to the rear of the small restaurant. Their waitress was leaning back against the counter. He read her body language. "Waitress looks like she could do with a little bit of luck thrown her way."

Collin shook his head. "Just when I think you're locked in your own little world…" He let his voice trail off.

Emmett took a packet of sugar and slipped it into his pocket to use later. He liked his coffee sweet and black. Sometimes there weren't enough packets to satisfy his craving.

"Just because I don't comment on them doesn't mean I don't notice things around me. Well, I've got FBI agents to badger and irritate the hell out of. Never realized what a tight-assed bunch they were."

"I guess you didn't take a mirror with you while you were up in those mountains." Collin never cracked a smile.

Emmett spared him a dark look. "Talk to

you tonight." Not waiting for a response, he walked out of the restaurant.

Pushing away his empty plate, Collin drained his second cup of coffee and put a twenty on top of Emmett's ten. He didn't have time for the waitress to write up the check. He had a few things to get to before he met with Lucy.

The thought of the latter made his blood move just a tad faster through his veins.

He pretended not to notice.

It took Collin a little less than an hour to reach his ultimate destination after he'd picked Lucy up at the medical examiner's. For the most part, the road leading from the jail where Jason had been kept to the maximum security prison was one that echoed of loneliness. Being on it made a man think of all the wrong turns his life had taken.

He wondered if any of these thoughts had occurred to Jason, or if he'd felt that he was just a victim of a fate that dealt in cruelty. That none of what had befallen him was his fault or a result of something he'd done.

By the time he reached the place where the van had gone off the side of the road, the win-

ter sun was waning in the sky. Parking his vehicle, he got out.

"You can stay in the car," he told Lucy. "It's
warmer."

She looked at him and he could almost
read her mind. There was no way she was
just going to sit here, twiddling her thumbs.
"Moving around will warm me up."

Lucy got out with a bounce that had long
since been missing in his step.

Shutting the door, she didn't bother lock-
ing it. She looked down at the skid marks the
transport van had left.

"What do you think made it go off the side
of the road like that?"

Since there were no signs of a dead animal
in the road and no one to tell them, Collin was
left to theories that might never be proven.

"Off the top of my head, I'd say a driver
with a knife to his throat might not be the saf-
est thing to have behind the wheel."

He moved around slowly, taking in the area.
Here and there, there were still some patches
of ice that hadn't completely melted. They
crunched with protesting groans beneath his
feet as he marked off where the vehicle had
gone off the road. He tried to envision what
had happened here.

The van had long since been taken away. Not so the skid marks where the tires had dug into the road as the van had gone careening off the main highway, into the ditch. The tire marks were going to be there for a long, long time.

Lucy followed Collin for a little while in silence. Finally she asked, "What is it you're looking for?"

He didn't bother to turn around. He was too busy examining the ground, the tiny shoots pushing their way up. Had they been here when the vehicle had crashed, he might have had something to go on.

"I don't know yet," he told her honestly. "Something," he murmured more to himself than to her. When he'd stopped at the morgue, he'd tried to talk her out of coming with him. But she'd been stubborn. As he'd known she would be.

He was looking for a lead. Anything. Something more than he'd gotten from the people he'd interviewed. He'd been so desperate he'd even run down the charitable organizations that Melissa Wilkes had joined in the last year. The people who ran the charities had nothing much to offer, except that it was becoming increasingly clear that Melissa had joined the organizations for the sole purpose of getting on Ryan's good side. Hoping to impress him.

Hoping to steal him from his wife.

That, Collin surmised, had brought about her demise more than anything. Jason wouldn't have looked kindly on having her flirt with the very man he was trying to bring down.

It had snowed shortly after the escape. The layers of ice had blocked things away from view. But the thaw had finally come. March had brought with it unusually warmer weather. It was by no means balmy, but for March, it was warm. Warm enough to melt the ice and to release whatever it might have been hiding.

The patch of weeds looked disturbed on one side. Collin squatted to get a closer look. The patch had been bent from the heel of a shoe. The snow that had fallen had preserved it.

"I think he might have gone this way at first," Collin offered.

It made sense. He'd head for the cover of trees himself to get out of sight. Into the brush. But where would Jason have stayed? It snowed within hours of the escape. Would he have tried to get back into town for shelter? Or had there been a halfway point for him, secluded in its earthiness?

Watching the ground carefully, he found

several more disturbances. Tracks hidden by the snow, but now exposed to the light.

Lucy kept out of his way, shadowing his movements. "It's like watching Daniel Boone at work," she commented softly.

He didn't know if she meant for him to hear that. "Don't you mean Davy Crockett?" The native of Tennessee was the more popular figure of the two.

"No, Daniel Boone," she repeated. "I came down with some kind of rare infection one summer when I was eleven while both my parents were stationed just outside of Rome. My father got me all these books to read. Read Daniel Boone's life story twice."

He couldn't help wondering what she was like then. That she liked to read pointed to someone who had difficulty reaching out. "Most kids would have watched TV."

"I read."

Collin was studying the ground around him intently. Looking up, Lucy shaded her eyes and surveyed the surrounding area. Her eyes narrowed and she tapped Collin on the shoulder.

He raised his head to look at her. "What?"

Rather than answer, she pointed in front of them. Into the heart of the forest.

There was a cave up ahead.

Chapter 10

"Damn it, he was here. How could they have missed it?" Collin fumed, shoving his fisted hands deep into his pockets.

It was the first time she'd seen Collin get angry. It wasn't exactly a heartwarming sight and it took Lucy aback for a moment. The Army Ranger's rugged face looked like a thunderstorm about to wreak havoc on the innocent countryside.

She could see him struggling to hold on to his temper. She couldn't help wondering how much more fearsome he could be if he let himself go.

Though she secretly didn't welcome the

venture, they had gone into the cave once they reached it. Within fifty feet of the mouth, there was evidence that someone had been here.

Squatting, Collin picked up a stick and slowly poked around in the ashes of what had once been a small campfire. The fire had long since been put out and grown cold. Discarded cans of food, their pop-tops not completely pulled off, lay strewn around beside empty plastic bottles that had once held water.

Standing over him, silently telling herself to breathe normally, Lucy unclenched her hands at her sides. To take her mind off her situation, she tried to second guess the thinking of the investigators who had been in the area before them.

"Maybe because this led into the forest and they assumed that, like any criminal, he was trying to put as much distance between himself and the police as possible, not holding up somewhere close by."

There was a comforter not too far from the campfire. She toed it, gingerly checking if there was anything left beneath.

There wasn't.

"According to the report," she recalled, "there were indications that he'd gone away from Red Rock, toward San Antonio. Going through the stream to lose his tracks." It seemed like a logical assumption to her.

Lucy looked around the inhospitable area. It was the last place she would have wanted to spend any time in the winter. She looked into the belly of the cave. It seemed to go on for at least a mile. Lucy stifled a shiver. No amount of money could have gotten her in any farther. Here, at least, there was light coming in. It looked pitch-black in there.

A thought occurred to her. "You know," she said suddenly, "until one of those cans or bottles are matched for prints, we're really not sure if he was even here. Maybe we've wandered in on the secret stash of some homeless man, or even a hermit, like your cousin was for a while."

Still squatting, Collin was staring at the cans. He shook his head. "No, it was Jason."

The way he said it, there was no room for debate. She glanced toward the cave entrance again, as if to assure herself that it was still there, still available to run through.

She was having trouble dragging air into her lungs. "How can you be so sure?"

"Because I know the way Jason thinks. Staying around here, near Red Rock, near Ryan's Double Crown Ranch, would be exactly what he *would* do." Using a corner of the comforter, he held up one of the cans for her perusal. "Besides, this is the way he always opened cans, even when he used a can opener. He never quite finished the job. He was always too impatient to get at what was inside. It's the way he lives his life. Impatiently."

It felt as if there was some kind of buzzing in her ears, winking sounds in and out. She was going to have to get out of here soon. Lucy struggled to look calm, if not actually feel calm.

"How well *do* you know him?" she asked. She had cousins somewhere. Two boys and a girl from her father's side of the family. Other than a few photographs taken at someone's birthday party when she was five, she had nothing to remember them by. She hadn't seen them since and wouldn't know any of them if she tripped over them. She and her parents had moved around far too much to promote any kind of family bond.

"Well enough when we were kids," Collin told her. But there was more at work here than that. "I know his type."

Now he was speaking professionally. "Part of your profiling abilities," she guessed.

He gave a vague nod of his head. It went

along with his unwillingness to talk about what he did or didn't do. What paths he took and those he refrained from taking. Even so, he had to admit that he'd found himself far more talkative with Lucy than he'd been with anyone for a very long time. The last person he'd had this kind of a rapport with had been his father.

Collin thought about August Jamison now. Maybe it was time to give him a call.

He glanced over his shoulder in Lucy's direction. She'd edged over a little closer to the mouth of the cave. Funny how being with this woman made him think about things like home and hearth. Things he wouldn't normally have given a second thought to, or even a first for that matter. He'd stopped even noticing things domestic since he'd attended Paula's wedding.

Lucy seemed to bring out a side of him that had been in the shadows so long, he was certain it didn't exist anymore.

The thought surprised him. He wasn't accustomed to feeling like a man. Wasn't accustomed to feeling like anything at all, except an Army Ranger.

Which was what he was, he reminded himself. And what he was doing here. Gathering intelligence to be sifted through later.

"Stay here," he told her in a low voice.

Long, thin nails of panic scratched at her throat. "Where are you going?"

He motioned toward the belly of the cave. Toward the darkness. "To make sure he isn't still hiding in there, watching us."

The time she stood there, waiting for Collin to emerge, straining to hear any telltale sounds of danger, seemed endless. Her eyes strained so hard, watching the darkness, she thought they were going to pop out of her head.

But finally he returned, slowly shaking his head. Jason wasn't here any longer.

Lucy began to turn on her heel, only to notice that he'd stopped by the campsite to pick something up. Trying to get her mind off the fact that the walls of the cave seemed to be narrowing, Lucy watched Collin as he took one of the empty bottles and carefully put it in a bag he pulled out of the deep pockets of his creased leather jacket.

When he rose to his feet, she looked at him curiously. Why just one? The area was littered with bottles and cans. "Aren't you going to take the rest of it in?"

"No, I'm leaving everything else just the

way we found it, in case he comes back," he explained. "There's bound to be some back-wash inside the bottle. That'll give us his DNA even if there are no prints on the bottle—which there probably are." Taking out his cell phone, he flipped it open. He needed to get in touch with Emmett. But as he began to press the first key, he frowned.

There was no signal.

He needed to get out in the open again. "C'mon." He waved her on. "Let's go outside again."

"Can't be fast enough for me," she murmured.

He'd noticed that she'd hesitated at the mouth of the cave just before they'd gone in. But when he'd told her that she didn't have to go with him, that she could stay behind, she'd squared her shoulders and said something about his leading the way.

"If there're any mountain lions around," she said, using the first thing that came to mind to call his attention away from her slip, "you can divert them from me."

It made Collin think of his conversation with Emmett, likening her to a mountain lion. Thinking about it now made it a little easier to disregard what was so plainly in front of him.

Now that he looked, he realized that her face was pale. Even in this light. "You're claustrophobic." It wasn't a question.

She began to deny it. After all, she saw claustrophobia as a weakness and she wasn't about weaknesses, just strengths. She'd always firmly believed that. If you were weak, they could hit you where you lived.

But then she blew out a breath and conceded. There seemed to be no point in lying.

"A little," she allowed. It was all she would admit to. "I don't break out in a cold sweat in elevators or small places, but—" she took another breath, because it was hard for her to own up to something like this "—I do feel a tightness in my chest."

Collin glanced at her chest and smiled to himself. The region looked pretty firm and tight from where he was standing.

The thought surprised him. He wasn't given to dwelling on physical attributes when they didn't figure into a case. He'd trained himself not to notice.

Or he thought he had.

Somehow his training was unraveling here. "Then, let's get out of here so that I can get a signal and you can get some decent air into your lungs."

Without thinking, he placed his hand against the small of her back. This time he noticed that she didn't stiffen, didn't pull back. He left his hand there.

Once outside, he called Emmett with news of the discovery.

Emmett sounded the most animated he'd heard him in a long time. "I'll get someone to post a guard around there, in case he comes back."

Collin glanced back at the mouth of the cave. "I don't think he will." His eyes passed over Lucy. Her color looked as if it was returning. He felt a little guilty, allowing her to go in.

"You never know," Emmett was saying. "Jason's arrogant enough to think that no one's discovered his hiding place. It can't hurt to have someone there, just in case."

Which meant, Collin surmised, that he was exchanging information with his fellow agents. "Sounds like they've welcomed you back into the fold."

"Not yet, not officially," Emmett contradicted. "Officially would put me some place other than here," he reminded his cousin. "Thanks for calling." The line went dead.

He'd forgotten that for a moment, Collin thought, closing his phone again. He'd been forgetting a lot of things lately. Ever since he'd hooked up with the bright young medical student, thoughts had been less than organized in his head.

He looked at her for a long moment, watching the way the winter sun tangled itself in her hair. He found himself wishing for things, wanting things, feeling the hollow spots inside of him become less so. "Do you have to be getting back?"

"No." He must have forgotten, Lucy thought. But then, why would he remember something that didn't have anything to do with the case? "I'm off for the rest of the day."

His eyes indicated the empty plastic water bottle. "What do you say to a late lunch after we drop this off to be analyzed?"

Lucy glanced at the sack he held. She wondered if he was just going through the motions because he figured that would be the best way to get her to do things for him, to help him with his case. After all, she represented his access to the forensic lab.

All the reasoning in the world didn't change her answer. "I say yes."

"Good." He smiled down into her face, resisting a very sudden, very real urge to kiss her again. "Because I'm hungry."

She looked at his lips for a moment, fighting back a strong wave of desire. So was she.

She was both relieved and saddened when he turned and started walking back to the car. With a suppressed sigh that held a myriad of emotions behind it, she quickly fell into place beside him.

There was no point in going into the office any longer. Ryan felt too weak to carry on the charade, too weak to maintain the facade of a man whose presence was essential for all the wheels of progress to continue turning in his various industrial empires.

Soon enough, according to the way he felt and what the doctors had said, those same wheels would have to turn without him.

To his credit, he'd made sure that the companies he headed would all go on smoothly when he was no longer there to helm them. He'd passed the reins on to younger people. Healthier people.

It was a strange thought that came to him in moments when the tumor was not assaulting him with waves of pain. Everything would continue when he was gone rather than abruptly stop.

It was what he wanted, and yet…

It was just his fear talking, he told himself. His fear of what lay beyond. He'd always been a man of strong, albeit quiet, religious convictions. He'd made peace with his Maker over this curve that had been thrown to him out of nowhere.

But there were times when he couldn't help feeling incredibly sad. The fact that he actually wasn't immortal, that he wasn't going to continue forever, would rise up suddenly out of the mists of his daily life and mock him.

He supposed that every man, every woman, carried with them the seeds of immortality merely by having children, by leaving a mark that they had passed this way. But still, it was a difficult concept to come to terms with. That one day he wouldn't open his eyes, wouldn't...

Continue.

The headaches were getting more frequent. Stronger. But he held out as long as he could against them, against taking any painkillers. The medication the doctor had prescribed to ease his pain made him feel mentally fuzzy and he didn't want to be fuzzy. He wanted to be able to absorb everything around him.

Even the presence of unexpected visitors like the young man sitting in front of him.

Ever since the news of his condition had

been made public, he'd had an incredible amount of people come through his house. But Garrett Wolff was not one of the ones he'd thought would come. Mainly because Garrett never stopped working.

The young man, who was senior vice president of the Expansion Division of Voltage Energy Company, reminded him a great deal of himself when he was younger. Not so much in looks. For one thing, the lanky thirty-two-year-old was of Nordic descent and had the blond hair—which he wore rather long— and blue eyes to prove it. No, it was Garrett's manner more than anything that brought back echoes of his own past to Ryan. A past when he'd felt invincible and entertained thoughts about forever.

As if realizing that he had lost the attention of the man he had come to pay his respects to, Garrett abruptly stopped talking. When Ryan looked at him, he apologized, "I'm tiring you out."

Ryan waved a hand that had become almost too heavy to manage. "No, really, I'm enjoying this," he protested.

"They told me you lie like a diplomat." Garrett's smile had a tinge of sadness to it.

The way everyone's did these days, Ryan thought. He saw it everywhere he went.

People who barely knew him personally now looked at him with sadness in their eyes. As if they were mourning with him. Mourning for this life that was slipping through his fingers like drops of water.

He'd always wanted to leave the world a better place than he'd found it. But truth be told, he really didn't want to leave it at all. Not for years to come. He felt he was still too young to die.

Too young to stop living.

The matter, he reminded himself, was out of his hands. All he could do was depart graciously and leave a lasting, dignified impression in his wake.

"Do not go gentle into that good night," the poet had said. But he was past that point. All he had left was gentility.

And dignity.

"Maybe I am a little tired," he allowed. He didn't want to make his guest uncomfortable and gave him a way out.

Garrett was on his feet instantly. He'd come to pay his respects to the most noble man he'd ever met. A man he'd tried to pattern his own life after. But he had no desire to wear Ryan out, to sap what little strength it appeared the once dynamic man had at his disposal.

Taking Ryan's hand in his, Garrett shook it. It surprised him and heartened him that Ryan's grip still felt strong. Given his deteriorating condition, it was nothing short of a miracle. But then, Ryan Fortune was all about miracles.

"I'd like to come by again," Garrett told him, "if that's all right with you."

Ryan smiled as the doorbell pealed in the distance. "Make it soon."

It wasn't a polite statement, it was a statement of fact. Later, Ryan knew, might be too late. He wouldn't be here.

Even as he sat here, surrounded by the outward signs of his success, his walls covered with framed photographs capturing him with various heads of corporations and charitable foundations he had given his energies to, he could feel life ebbing away, passing out of his body with each breath he took.

His housekeeper appeared in the doorway of the den, peering into the room as if afraid to disturb him even for a moment. She knocked softly on the door frame.

Ryan didn't make the effort to turn around. He knew who it was. His Lily never knocked.

She entered a room like sunshine, bathing a room with her essence.

"Yes?"

"Mr. Ryan, Miss Kyra is here to see you."

At the mention of the new visitor's name, Garrett involuntarily stiffened.

Kyra Fortune, Ryan's much younger cousin, was his Associate V.P. What's more, the statuesque platinum-blonde was out for his job.

Nothing had been said, of course, but he could smell it the way only a man who had pulled himself up by his bootstraps out of the soul-numbing abyss of poverty could.

He had a very strong instinct for self-preservation. He wouldn't be where he was if he didn't. Kyra, on the other hand, was a child of privilege, who undoubtedly felt entitled to anything that caught her fancy, however fleetingly. And the top position in the company had done just that.

Well, she couldn't have his position. He'd worked damn hard to get here and no self-absorbed, spoiled brat was going to wrestle it away from him, even if she thought she was entitled to.

"Now it's really time for me to go," he murmured, intending the comment to be more to himself than to Ryan.

Ryan looked at him with interest. His body was turning on him, but his mind, whenever the headaches left him alone, was still sharp.

"You and Kyra work together, don't you?"

Ryan made it sound like a harmonious association. Garrett thought of the battle of wits that had gone on between them almost from day one.

"I'd say only in the loosest sense of the word, Mr. Fortune."

His semi-disclaimer brought a wan smile to the other man's lips. Whatever the cause, it was good to see Ryan smile, Garrett thought.

At that moment Kyra breezed in, a ray of confidence in four-inch heels.

"Ryan, how are you?" she asked, and then she stopped short.

The housekeeper hadn't mentioned that there was someone else in the room with her cousin, much less that it was her boss, Garrett Wolff. As far as she knew, the man kept his rather attractive nose pressed close to the grindstone twenty-four hours a day.

Kyra pressed her lips together, suppressing a sound of deep displeasure at her discovery. It was self-righteous people like Wolff who kept her from advancing. They all thought that she only wanted to get somewhere because of her name.

If they only knew...

Her name was more of a burden than anything else, keeping her down because everyone seemed bent on showing her that being a Fortune meant nothing. They were so dedicated to their goal that they tended to overlook her accomplishments. All they did was focus in on the fact that she was a Fortune and "that's not going to get you anywhere around here, so don't expect it to."

Garrett had said those very words to her at their initial meeting.

She never forgot it and it made her twice as determined to best him at his own game. Just to show him she could. Not because she was a Fortune, but because she was Kyra, someone who got what she was after and wasn't afraid to work to get it.

Her gaze frosted over as she looked at the man she had to face on a daily basis, but her words were intended for Ryan.

"Oh. I'm sorry, I didn't realize that there would be anyone here with you."

Garrett returned the cold look in kind. She was like a tick in his side, constantly gnawing away at his flesh. Trying to make him back away to give her a clear shot at things.

Over his dead body.

Or hers.

"I was just leaving," he informed her.

"Good," she said with a bit too much feeling. Then she smiled as she looked at Ryan, pretending to temper her words. "It'll give me some time alone with my favorite cousin."

Garrett shook his head. How could someone like Ryan be related to someone who could easily be mistaken for Satan's daughter?

"Thanks for coming," Ryan said to Garrett as the latter took his leave. Amusement curved his mouth, although he doubted that either of the other parties was aware of the reason.

From his vantage point, he could observe that there was enough electricity within the room to run a large generator for a month and a half. Too bad he wasn't going to be around to see how this all played out, Ryan thought with a twinge of sadness.

Yes, he thought as Kyra sat beside him, life was going to continue, even if he was no longer around to participate.

Chapter 11

He took her to the small Mexican café that claimed to serve the best chili this side of the border. Not being an expert, Collin had no way of knowing if they lived up to their claim, but it was better than just satisfactory and Lucy seemed to enjoy it.

He enjoyed watching her enjoy it.

He found the thought, when it dawned on him, a little unnerving and more than slightly disconcerting. He took note of other people's reaction to things, cataloging them for future use whenever he was called upon to create a profile of the man or woman he found himself tracking.

But this went into a file all its own. A file marked "Lucy." A file without a purpose, other than to exist for its own sake. And to give him pleasure should he peruse through it.

Upbraiding himself accomplished nothing, so he stopped trying and went back to enjoying.

They lingered over lunch a great deal longer than either of them was accustomed to. To Lucy, lunch was anything a vending machine might cough up, or, on rare occasions, the sandwich she thought to bring, badly wrapped in aluminum foil and slightly misshapen. For Collin, meals never had that much structure to them. He ate when he was hungry if something was available.

Eating at a prescribed hour had not meant anything to him since he'd left his father's house. But a great many things were now being reshuffled, resetting themselves in the scheme of things.

Like slipping into a groove that he had never quite occupied before.

Since before reaching puberty, learning the lesson at his father's knee, he'd been a man's man for so long, he'd forgotten what it was like to feel something around a woman.

Or if he even could.

But this woman was unlocking doors, opening windows, freshening quarters of his being that had become stale with stagnant air.

She made him somehow feel, just by being with her, by listening to her talk, that sunshine had taken down the "vacancy" sign and moved in.

As they talked, he discovered that they had things in common. It turned out that they were both close to their fathers. Both learned at an early age to rely chiefly on themselves for whatever emotional sustenance they needed, she because either one or both of her parents were usually posted somewhere away from her and he because as much as he loved his father, the man was usually busy. For as long as Collin could remember, August Jamison had been attached to the CIA in a capacity that best used his psychological training.

Lucy asked more than her share of questions. Each time he tried to turn the conversation back toward her, she somehow managed to field whatever he asked, then sent the conversation right back to him.

Amused by what he felt was a clever psychological sleight of hand, he tried again and again to bring it back around to her.

"Do you get to see him much?" he asked as

the bill arrived. He placed his credit card over the check on the off-white tray.

Preparing to leave, Lucy slipped her arms into the jacket she'd draped over the back of her chair. "My father? More now that he's retired and moved here to be close to me."

She remembered how surprised she'd been to discover that they were practically neighbors. And that her father wanted to be her friend as well as her parent. It was then she began to think of him as a person, not just a parental figure.

And realized that he was lonely now that he no longer had her mother's return to look forward to.

"Not as much as either one of us would like," she added. An ironic smile played on her lips. "Now I'm the busy one. I don't think he much cares for the other side of the coin, but he understands, which is good." She gave a small, careless shrug of her shoulders as she finished pulling on her jacket. "Doesn't assuage the guilty feelings, but it helps."

The waitress returned with the tray again. Collin quickly signed the credit card receipt, then tore off his copy. He tucked it into the pocket of his jacket. "Guilty feelings?"

She nodded. She'd been surprised to experience a few of those. "That there aren't enough hours in the day to make time for those we love."

He looked at Lucy for a long moment before telling her, "Sometimes we arrange it that way without realizing it."

She tried to read between the lines and couldn't. His eyes were deadly serious. Too serious. She tried to lighten the mood. "Oh, am I going to be subjected to your keen insight?"

He took a breath, then let it go. "I was referring to myself."

Her eyes narrowed. The focus took on a different direction. "Oh?"

"Actually," he recalled, "that was what my fiancée said to me."

Something went very cold within her. It was the first time he'd mentioned another woman. He was engaged. Then why had he kissed her, damn it? It was Jeff all over again. Jeff, who she'd spent so many hours daydreaming about, making plans for the future. Jeff, who, in moments of weakness, she'd thought of giving her seventeen-year-old virtue to.

Her mouth felt as though it was filled with hot sand. "Fiancée?"

He nodded. "Yeah. She said it to me just before she married my best friend. Said she was tired of waiting for me to make time for her. To 'wake up and smell the coffee,' as she so creatively put it." He shrugged philosophically. "Instead, I woke up to smell the ashes." Irony hovered on his lips as they curved. "I was just in time to be too late."

Lucy had been all set to walk out, mentally calling herself seven kinds of a fool. She called herself that anyway, for jumping to a conclusion. But once burned with a poker, it was hard not to jump when she thought she saw one being raised.

She did her best to mask her reaction and her thoughts. She tried to place herself in his position. The same position she'd occupied when Jeff had told her he was marrying another woman, the one who was carrying his baby. "I'm sorry."

Again, he shrugged, uncomfortable with the subject and a little mystified that he was responsible for bringing it up. He only had himself to blame. "My father's a great believer in fate. He says if something is meant to happen, it will."

She laughed softly, unaware that the sound wove its way into his belly. "That's a good excuse not to do anything," she pointed out.

"Yeah, it is."

And he had already done too much, he thought, annoyed with his lack of discipline. There was no need to involve himself with this woman beyond the basics. She was in the M.E.'s office, she'd alerted him to certain things about the case. For that, he was grateful, but he couldn't allow that to be an excuse to see more of her. She had no place in this investigation.

Nor did she have any place in any corner of his life. There were no vacancies in his life, he told himself. At least, none he was willing to rent out.

He'd always known when to retreat, and this was definitely that time. "I'd better be getting back to work," he told her. "I'll drop you off at the M.E.'s office on my way so you can pick up your car."

"Where are you off to next?" She wanted to know.

"A few odds and ends I need to see to." Collin paused, then looked at her significantly. "And a promise to keep."

She wasn't sure what to make of the expression on his face. He was suddenly so serious again. And yet there was compassion in his eyes. The man completely mystified her. "Oh?"

His eyes met hers. The butterflies in her stomach found their wings turning to lead, no longer moving quickly. No longer moving at all.

"The one I made to you," he said.

She was drawing a blank. He was the last man in the world to make a woman a promise. Besides, except when they'd kissed, they hadn't been like a man and woman around each other at all. At least, he hadn't.

"I don't recall…"

"About your mother." He'd made some progress in that area, acting on his promise the very next day after he'd made it. "A friend said he might have something for me this afternoon."

Suddenly alert, she was ready to jump to her feet. "Can I come with you?"

The area was classified. Even with a visitor's badge, there was no way she could get in. Collin shook his head. "Afraid not. But if I come up with anything, I'll give you a call."

She hated the sound of the phone in the evening. That was how she'd received the initial news about her mother. Her father had called her immediately. She would have rather waited until she could have sunk into his arms, until they could have comforted each other in person. Instead she stood there, clutching a telephone receiver. Numb from the chest down.

"Why don't you stop by instead?" Lucy suggested, rising to her feet. "I'd rather get news face-to-face. The phone's so impersonal."

He stood, then went to pull Lucy's chair back for her. "There might not be anything more than you already know."

In her heart, she knew there was more than her mother just getting killed "in the line of duty." More than just that she had gotten caught in the cross fire of two battles raging between two warring factions of the same chaotic Third World country. Her mother would have been better utilized than that.

"I have a feeling there is," she said quietly. She blew out a breath. "And then I have to make up my mind whether or not to tell my father."

Collin thought of the world that he usually dealt in. "He might already know."

She shook her head. Her father had caught a plane and come to her dorm the day after he'd called. They'd spent the day remembering things about her mother. He far more than she.

"Unlike you, he's very easy to read. If my father knew more than he initially told me, I would have seen it in his eyes. And gotten it out of him," she added with no attempt at bravado. It was just the way things were. "He's not too good when it comes to keeping secrets. I think he sees them as lies. And it's not in his nature to lie." She'd often thought of her father as a gentle soldier, if there was such a thing. He was a big man, but he'd never been anything more than gentle and kind as far as she was concerned. "My mother was the clam," she added with a bemused smile on her lips.

"I'll come over," Collin promised.

They wove their way through the small dining area to the front of the restaurant. He noticed that Lucy no longer pulled away when he placed his hand to the small of her back. And noticed, too, that he rather liked the feeling that softly tiptoed through him while he had his hand against her back, guiding her out. Liked the subtle feeling of being part of two.

Not a couple, of course, but still, not quite alone either…

Dangerous ground, he warned himself. But then, he'd never shied away from crossing unsafe terrain before. And at his age, he was too old to learn new tricks.

Which was exactly why nothing was going to come of the feelings that were trying to push their way through like first spring grass through frozen ground.

He'd do well to remember that, Collin counseled himself.

As the cold air hit them upon walking outside the restaurant, Collin wondered if he was going to wind up walking out onto thin ice, wisdom notwithstanding.

Or if it was going to turn out to be solid and would bear his weight.

"Well, there you are, nestled in your chair and giving one magnificent impersonation of a slug," Vanessa Fortune Kincaid announced as she breezed into the den. The room was bathed in light, catching the morning sun's rays and hoarding them like a miser anticipating forty days of rain. She bent over her father, who was sitting in a recliner, and kissed his cheek. It felt unsettlingly cool to her lips, she thought. "The day's bright and beautiful for a change. Why don't we celebrate by going out for lunch?"

Vanessa was trying her best to be brave. For both their sakes. But they both knew that the cheer was little more than just a charade. That she knew just how badly he was doing and he knew she knew.

Still, clinging to the game made them strong. Kept dignity in place.

Not that Vanessa gave a damn about dignity, but she knew it was important to the man she'd loved with all her heart since the day she'd been born.

She made a point of stopping by the house where she'd grown up with her four siblings as often as she could, sadly aware that one day, all too soon, she was going to walk through that front door knowing that she wouldn't be able to find Ryan Fortune somewhere within one of the rooms. That his huge, larger-than-life presence would no longer fill the house.

No longer fill her life.

She was married, and dearly loved Devin, but her father had been the first man she'd ever loved.

Her mouth curved now as she remembered the adage: you never quite got over your first love. For her, it would always be true.

It killed her to see this vibrant, dynamic man reduced to a shell of his former self, ravaged by a brain tumor that allowed him no peace, consuming his energy, his essence.

As always, Vanessa had come to fight with the unseen enemy, trying her best to help her father rally one more time. And she would continue to do the very same thing each time she saw him. The way she saw it, each day he woke was a victory. And she was here to collect another victory.

But Ryan Fortune, once the toast of both coasts, able to go on for more than two days straight without a wink of sleep and still dance with his wife, shook his head slowly to the invitation his daughter extended.

"Sorry, princess, I'm afraid I'll have to take a rain check on lunch with you. I'm not up to slaying dragons today."

Suppressing a sigh, she dragged a chair over to his. She hadn't seen him on his feet in several days. It was as if her father were rapidly deteriorating right in front of her eyes.

She tried not to think about it. Or what lay ahead of them.

"Okay, no dragon slaying," she allowed. "How do you feel about wounding a lizard?"

He laughed. Vanessa could always make him laugh and he was grateful to her for that. "Maybe you should get started without me."

Vanessa pretended to sigh and rolled her eyes. "Oh, Daddy, you really know how to weasel out of things, don't you?"

Ryan looked at his daughter fondly. "I can

remember a sunny-eyed little girl who could give me lessons in that."

She'd been a handful when she was younger. Not bad, just incredibly mischievous. She knew all the stories by heart. "I grew up."

The smile that crossed his lips was fleeting and mostly sad, even though he tried his best not to be maudlin around his wife and children. But the mantle weighed heavily on him. "And I grew old."

She was nothing if not fiercely loyal, fiercely protective. "No, not you, Daddy. Not you. Older, maybe, but not old. You're the youngest man I know."

He interpreted that the only way he knew how. "Worn out your husband already, have you?"

There was a twinkle in her father's eye. Vanessa cherished it as she laughed in reply. "No, Devin's still got some mileage left in him."

Ryan nodded his head. More than just some, he thought. "More power to him. Knew Devin was the right man for you the second I laid eyes on him. Takes a hell of a man to keep up with you, 'Nessa."

"It should." Taking her father's hand in hers,

she cradled it as she looked at him meaningfully. "I was spoiled by the best."

Governors and senators had bestowed words of praise on him during his lifetime. It never pleased him as much as hearing kind words from his children. They were a man's true legacy and a test of his mettle.

"I don't know about the best," he said slowly, fighting off a wall of pain, "but I did spoil you. You and your sister and brothers." And then he smiled. "Best time of my life."

She pretended to lower her voice and move closer. "Don't let Lily hear you say that."

At the mention of his third wife's name, Ryan's wan smile grew stronger. He'd loved Lily for a very long time. But fate had arranged things so that their paths first had to go in different directions before they were finally allowed to cross again, permanently this time.

Initially, Lily had gone on to marry someone else, and so had he. Twice. Once to the mother of his children and once, in his grief, to a woman who had taken advantage of the sorrow in his heart. He discounted everything he'd had to endure on the journey that had brought him to Lily because he finally had Lily by his side. And even though the time they had together proved to be relatively short, he was grateful for that. Grateful for every scrap he could get.

The pain was worsening again, reminding him that it was never far away. That it was the jailer and he the prisoner. He struggled not to let it show on his face. He didn't want his daughter's pity. Only her company.

"I've been a very fortunate man," he told her. "Having all of you, your mother and Lily in my life."

Vanessa hated it when he sounded like that. As if he was about to close the book.

"Daddy, don't talk as if it's over. It's not. Tomorrow they might discover something that'll destroy this awful thing that's sapping your strength." She was an optimist, she always had been. But even she had her limits and she was frighteningly close to it. So much so that it was a struggle not to cry. "They might even be coming up with it in some far-off laboratory even as we sit here talking."

He smiled at her. Vanessa was his ray of sunshine. Ever hopeful. And he loved her for it. Even though there was no foundation for what she was saying. They both knew that. His days were limited.

"They might," he allowed. "And then again—"

"Don't go there, Daddy," she ordered, her voice stern. At the breaking point. "I won't let you go there." Vanessa looked at her father, the tears she was trying unsuccessfully to hold back shimmering in her eyes. "I won't let you go."

He ran his hand through her hair, the way he used to when she was a little girl. But now the effort was almost too much for him. The pain was taking on proportions again, bringing with it bursts of stars and lights that clouded his vision.

"I know, princess, but sometimes what we want doesn't matter." His eyes searched her face. "I'm very proud of you and I want you to go on and have a good life with Devin, understand? Have it for me. And I'll always be with you." He tried his best to smile, to look like the man he'd been such a short time ago. "Never more than a whisper away."

It was what he'd said to her when she'd been a little girl, afraid of the dark, afraid to fall asleep in her room for fear that the monsters would get her. He'd promised her that he would come if she needed him, that all she needed to do was to call and he'd be there. Never more than a whisper away.

Vanessa thought her heart was going to break as she nodded.

Lucy glanced at her watch. She'd done it so many times since she'd come home from the lab this afternoon, she'd lost count, and the butterflies in her stomach were mocking her.

After all, Military Man hadn't said he was definitely coming over, only that he'd stop by if he had something. *If* he had something. So why was she straining so hard to hear a knock on the door or the sound of the doorbell fading away?

She told herself that it was because she was anxious about any illuminating news regarding her mother, but she knew that was only an excuse. She wasn't listening for a messenger or for an informant; she was listening for the man who had succeeded in breaking through the steel barriers around her thoughts. All her senses were keenly alert so she could hear the advance of a man who had managed to somehow weave his way into the pattern of her thoughts.

And he had done it with just one damn kiss.

A performance Collin'd had opportunities to repeat and never did, she reminded herself tersely.

But reminding herself of that didn't cause her pulse to slow or her hands to lose the slightly damp feeling they'd attained.

Annoyed with herself, she wiped her hands along her jeans.

How stupid could she get? She was acting like some kind of teeny-bopper. Even then, she hadn't acted that way. God knew she'd been uprooted time and again, faced new situations frequently, and she'd never felt more than mildly nervous on each occasion. What would be, would be. Her calm had been her gift.

But for some reason, that kind of one-on-one hadn't felt nearly as personal as this did.

She was being an idiot, she upbraided herself.

And then she heard it. She really heard it this time, rather than thought she did like the last two times she'd raced to answer the door only to find herself staring off into empty space.

Last time, she promised herself as she crossed to the door.

She didn't care if she thought she heard the Mormon Tabernacle Choir singing "Amazing Grace" on her doorstep, she wasn't going to answer her door. Three times and then you're out. That included her. And Military Man, she tagged on firmly.

Lucy yanked open the door.

And there he was, standing on her doorstep. Military Man.

Chapter 12

Lucy tried to read his expression and failed. "You know something?"

The nod was barely perceptible.

Much like she imagined Collin probably gave in response to a query from any of the operatives who crossed his path. He was not a man who was given to any sort of an emotional display.

But even so, something made her believe that beneath the rugged exterior, there was a man who felt, who bled and cared. Why else would he be here now, with information for her when there was nothing in it for him? Other than her words of gratitude.

Collin walked in. Lucy closed the door behind him and waited, holding her breath. When he didn't say anything, she couldn't stand it any longer.

"What?" she pressed, moving out in front of him so that he was forced to face her.

The tail end of a debate raged within him. Ever since he'd agreed to come down here to help Emmett, he'd been doing things against his nature. To get what Lucy wanted to know, he'd pulled strings, called in favors. Digging into the past was never straightforward.

Right now he was violating half a dozen rules, all of which could have gotten him dismissed immediately, if not jailed indefinitely. The right military thing to do was to keep his mouth shut. To never have investigated at all. But the right moral thing was a different matter. It wasn't as if she was looking to trade on the information. This was about family, about her mother, and she had a right to know. When it came to family, he drew a line in the sand. She had a right to know, he thought again. Just as Emmett had a right to try to track down his brother.

Unbuttoning his jacket, he shed it and tossed it over the back of the butterscotch-leather love seat that served as her sofa. He loosened his tie and undid the top button of his denim shirt, as if the words couldn't come out if he were still formal.

His eyes were on hers as he told her. "Your mother was killed while working deep undercover. Her assignment was to guard one of the Saudi princes who was involved in a peace negotiation. There was an assassination attempt. She took the bullet that was meant for him."

Lucy's eyes widened as he spoke. She remembered reading about the incident when it happened. There were pictures in the newspaper of the prince and his bodyguards. They were all men.

"The account said that no one got hurt except for one of the prince's mistresses." The words dribbled from her lips, each one slower than the last as the import of what she was saying sank in.

Again, Collin nodded. He was watching her for signs of a stressed reaction. This wasn't just a tidbit he was tossing her. This was something that would shake up her world, cause it to reform.

"That was your mother's cover. To be truthful, I don't know if the prince even knew that she was an operative."

Lucy stared at him, unable, unwilling to assimilate the implications. If the prince didn't know her true identity, her true function, then as his mistress— No, not her mother. Maybe the newspapers just called her that because that was what they'd been told, but not what was true.

She looked to Collin for help, for support. "Then she…"

He knew exactly where she was going with this, exactly what was on her mind. It was as if her thoughts flashed across his own mind the instant she began talking. But he couldn't lie to her, even though he knew that was what she wanted. Because the truth was too bitter to swallow.

"I have no way of knowing that, Lucy. None of us does. Probably the only one who could answer your question, truthfully, is your mother."

Her shoulders sagged beneath the weight of the information he'd just given her.

"Not much chance of that," Lucy murmured. She let out a ragged breath as she made up her mind. "I'm not telling my father." There was no need for him to have this information. "He thinks of her as a hero, anyway. No reason to make him wonder if the woman he loved was faithful to him or if her duty to her country had her putting aside her marriage vows." It was bad enough that she would always wonder about it, wonder without ever really having a chance to find out one way or another.

She stopped focusing on herself, on what this meant to her and what it did to the image of her mother that she carried around with her. Instead she turned her attention to the man who had gotten this for her against all odds. Who'd risked a great deal because of a promise he'd made to her.

She placed her hand on his. "Thank you. I realize that you got this at a cost."

One broad shoulder rose and fell in a dismissive gesture. "I gave you my word."

Which he prized a great deal, she thought. It just went to show her the measure of this man. At this moment he could have asked her anything and she would have tried to do it for him, tried to obtain it for him. Maybe that was even the purpose behind all this, she thought, and maybe later on she'd see it that way. But right now that speculation didn't take away from the magnitude of what he'd done for her.

"You could have said that you couldn't find out," she pointed out.

By his expression, she could see that the

thought hadn't even crossed Collin's mind. "But that would be lying."

Her lips curved slightly. "I imagine you occasionally lie in your line of work."

His eyes didn't leave hers. She felt as if they were delving into her. Speaking to something that didn't need words. "Not to someone who counts."

Lucy looked at him for a long moment, so many things stirring up inside of her she couldn't even begin to count, couldn't begin to sort them out. She'd always thought of herself as never needing anyone, not in that way. And yet, it didn't quite ring true, especially not at this moment. She didn't want to be alone inside of it.

"And am I someone who counts?"

He brushed back the hair that was falling to her eyes before he could stop himself. His fingertips lightly grazed her skin. "You know you are."

The breath she'd taken felt as if it had jagged edges that were rubbing against her throat, leaving wounds. "Right now I know very little. And the little I know seems to have gotten shaken up."

He felt the desire to comfort her, to erase the vulnerable look he saw in her eyes. He knew he should suppress it, but somehow, he didn't get around to it.

Collin lifted her chin, guilt at being the source of her pain filleting him. "Then I shouldn't have told you."

"No, you should have." Even as a child, she hated not knowing things. The mystery that always seemed to surround her mother drove her crazy. Every time she asked where her mother was off to, there'd be just the slightest bit of hesitation before Margaret Gatling would answer. Now she knew why. Because her mother was lying. And didn't want to. Not to her. But there'd been no choice. "It's better if I know."

Not from where he was standing, Collin thought. She looked like a woman whose soul had been stolen. "Better how?"

There was no way she could explain. She tried to smile. "Just better."

He wasn't sure if he believed her, but there was no point in debating it. It was best to let this die. "Then I'm glad I told you."

She knew how difficult it must have been to get the information. She only hoped he hadn't accidentally raised any red flags with his inquiry. She didn't want to be the reason for anything bad happening to him. "And risked court-martial?"

His mouth curved. "Only if you turn me in. And you wouldn't do that."

Not even if she was tortured. But he didn't know that about her, about how steadfast she was, how loyal she could be, Lucy thought.

She hadn't thought about that in a long time, her loyalty. The last person she'd offered it to, albeit silently, had rejected it and married someone else.

"How do you know?" she pressed, wanting to know if he was just talking, or if there was something within her that spoke to him.

He looked at her for a long moment, his eyes saying things to her his mouth couldn't. Her breath caught in her throat.

"I just know," he told her softly.

The pull between them grew stronger, more demanding. "Instincts?" Lucy asked, the word shimmering between them as she rose up on her toes, winding her arms around his neck.

"Something like that," Collin allowed, hardly aware that he was speaking at all. He was aware only of the warm body that was against his.

He closed his arms around her and pulled Lucy to him as he brought his mouth down on hers. He kissed her the way he'd been longing to ever since the last time. Ever since he'd met her.

Maybe even ever since the beginning of time.

He likened the sensation to the first thing that came to mind. For him, it was like being in the center of a mine field, with every single mine going off at the same time. It was terrifying and yet somehow almost exhilarating at the same time. Because he was still alive to bear witness to what was happening.

It was the way he'd lived a good deal of his life away from the States.

But this time the exhilaration, the rush, had a sweetness to it, an intoxicating aura that had him embracing everything that he knew, in his heart, was dangerous to his peace of mind.

To his very state of being.

What he was feeling now, what he was doing now, with someone like her, had no place in the life he led. Oh, the physical part could. He'd had his encounters with the opposite sex, although not with nearly the frequency of some of the other men he knew. He had no driving need to vent his manhood, to celebrate a win, a night, a beer, by finding a willing woman and mixing body fluids only to wake up the next morning and not remember anything, least of all a face. Things usually needed to have more meaning for him than that. The times he had had sex with a woman, it was because a chemistry had drawn him to it.

But even those encounters never lasted more than the night.

He'd resisted taking this woman in his arms because he'd sensed that there was more than just chemistry at work. More than just her reminding him, physically, of Paula. Lucy Gatling appealed to his mind, to his senses. And that was very dangerous. Because he didn't want her to. Didn't want to find himself needing her at some future date. If you needed, you were vulnerable. And that was the first step to destruction in his line of work.

He needed to operate on a level as close to a machine as possible.

But all that was logic and he wasn't feeling very logical tonight. There'd been something in her eyes, as he'd told her about her mother, that had somehow burrowed through all the barriers he'd erected, all the logic, all the locks that were in place. Burrowed through them with a diamond-tipped drill and left him at the center, naked and wanting.

Wanting her.

Framing her face in his hands, he tilted her head up toward him. His mouth slanted over hers again and again, as his body heated to a temperature hot enough to melt iron.

But he'd been a soldier for too long, instilled with discipline too long, to merely take what he felt—no, what he *knew*—was being offered to him. Even with this phase, he proceeded with the caution that had governed most of his adult life. Testing waters before diving straight into the swirling currents.

Collin dragged the palms of his hands up along her sides, grazing her breasts like the spring breeze along rose petals. Her moan echoed against his lips. Inflamed, he moved his hands in closer, cupping her breasts. He couldn't recall ever feeling anything so soft, even through the fabric barriers.

He could feel the heat charging from Lucy's body into his own. Could feel her twist against him with an urgency that was unexpected and that generated the same urgency within him.

His answers were given.

With steady hands that belied the degree of turmoil within him, he undid the buttons on her blouse, parting the material. His probing fingers felt her skin. The wired, push-up bra she wore presented her breasts to him like a silken offering.

Excitement roared through him at the speed of sound.

When he moved his palms over her flesh, her moan almost undid him, the soft sound hitting him in the center of his very core.

It unsettled him, the degree with which he wanted her. He wasn't familiar with it, with this need that sent flame throwers through him.

He tasted her desire. Tasted her surrender. And his mind spun around madly, not from the power, but from the sheer excitement he felt.

Lucy had always thought, given her strength of character, given the independence she'd carved out for herself early on and the principles she'd held so dear, that she would be able to resist anything. Especially this. That she'd be able to walk away from sex with no more than a backward glance. Damn, but she had no idea she could be so very wrong about herself.

After all, sex had been Jeff's undoing and it had ended her own dreams of being with him. There were consequences for coming this far, for allowing things to happen. But try as she might, as her mind swirled like a wild kaleidoscope, shooting out beams of color every-where, she couldn't think of a one of them.

All she knew at this very moment in time was that this sensation was something she'd only imagined before. Imagined and done a poor job of it at that. Because the reality of it was so much more.

Every part of her was vibrating wildly. Wanting more. Wanting him. It was as if suddenly, after twenty-six years, her body had declared its own independence, unshackled itself from the principles she'd held dear. Announcing, by the very act, that it had wants and needs and was going to find a way to satisfy them.

It was as if all of her had gone on automatic pilot, proceeding into uncharted waters by instincts she never knew she possessed.

She shivered, not with cold but with anticipation, as each article of clothing left her body. And as Collin undressed her, she did the same to him. Except that her hands, damn them, were far less steady than his. He was the professional and she was the vestal virgin.

It was such an accurate description, it almost made her laugh out loud.

She tried to absorb everything, every nuance, every movement, and press it between the pages of her mind. Collin was proceeding as if this was all commonplace to him—and why shouldn't it be? He was a worldly soldier and she, no matter what she told herself, was still the sheltered virgin.

Virginity had been her badge of courage, her shield. She didn't want it anymore. She didn't want to be a virgin if it meant not being with him tonight. Consciously or unconsciously, Lt. Collin Jamison was the one to whom she'd chosen to give her virginity.

The magnitude of the offering intruded into her thoughts even as her body temperature continued to rise. She couldn't wait to give him her gift. And she only prayed that he would accept it in the spirit it was given and not be disappointed because she was so woefully inexperienced. What she lacked in knowledge she hoped she made up for with spirit.

Collin was determined to give her pleasure. Everything he did, he received back tenfold. With each sigh, each moan, every twist of her body against his, his own excitement rose, increasing to almost unbearable heights. In one swift movement he picked her up and carried her to her bed, where he lay her against the silky comforter. He quickly joined her there.

He had no idea how he continued to hold himself in check when he wanted only to bury himself within her.

With restraint that had been drummed into him, Collin explored her body with his fingers, with his mouth, memorizing and being mesmerized at the very same time. He savored the slightly different taste of her as his tongue made her belly quiver, the sensitive area at the inside of her elbow dance, and her breath grow increasingly shorter when he kissed the hollow of her throat.

Each moment made the anticipation grow. And when he couldn't hold back any longer, when he felt it wasn't humanly possible to wait another second to have her, Collin pulled himself up over her. Watching her eyes, he parted her legs with his knee and drove himself into her with a force that was beyond his power to temper.

The cry against his mouth was not just one filled with pleasure. There was a whimper of pain woven into it. The latter registered at the very same moment that he realized he'd encountered resistance at the most basic level. Not because she was small, or because of any last-minute hesitation on her part, but because he'd come across a physical barrier and had gone through it before he was fully aware that it was there.

He would have pulled back to look at her quizzically, to ask what was hovering on his mind, but even now the whimper had faded and a rhythm had been struck. A rhythm that came from her as her hips began to move. It overtook him until it became all one and the same. They were joined, one, and no matter what had come before, it was too late to stop, to pull away. Collin could only tangle his fate with hers and race for the summit where the climax came, rocking him, cleaving him to her, shuddering its way through his body and holding it tightly in its grasp.

Collin held her in his arms the way he'd never held anyone before. As if letting go would send them both falling over the side of an abyss, never to surface.

But eventually the euphoria lifted, the excitement receded into the shadows, and he was left with nothing but reality.

It was so stark, it jarred his teeth. He turned his head to look at her as she lay nestled against him. He felt like an invader, a thief, taking what had never belonged to him.

"You're a virgin."

Here it came, she thought. It wasn't as if

she'd hoped to fool him. Nor was it something she was ashamed of. It was a state she'd elected to remain in. Until now.

"Yes," she said quietly, hugging her bravado to her, "I know."

Anger for not somehow knowing, for not somehow divining that fact, smoldered within his breast. "But— Damn it, you're a virgin."

He was up, on his elbow, looming over her. She felt at a disadvantage. All she had was her sheer nerve.

"We've already established that," she reminded him with a blasé attitude she could only summon from memory. "You say it as if it's a sin."

She watched as his expression hardened. Was he angry at her for not telling him ahead of time? As if she could have done that. "No, but it's a sin to take that from you."

She knew all the arguments to back up his words, had given the arguments to herself with ease whenever she'd been remotely tempted. And it had always been enough for her. Not this time. Because this time she'd wanted him with an unnerving fierceness.

"Why?" she asked.

He blew out a breath, feeling cornered, feeling as if he'd done something wrong. "Because a woman's first time is supposed to be with someone who matters."

"It was," she told him quietly. "You do."

Damn it, he didn't want her thinking those kinds of things about him. Despite their backgrounds, they came from two different worlds.

"Lucy—"

It wasn't panic she saw in his eyes; she was sure he had spent years training not to give that emotion away. But she thought she knew the male mind, knew the way it thought. And he probably thought that she was thinking hearts and flowers and wedding dates.

"Don't worry about it, Military Man," she told him tersely. "I'm a product of two pragmatic people, one of whom turned out to be Mata Hari." That was going to take a lot of getting used to. "I'm not about to go running to my father and beg for a shotgun wedding just because we made love."

Love, she thought, not sex. Love. It helped, somehow, to call it that even though she knew he didn't think of it in those terms.

He studied her face, trying his best to disentangle himself from the guilt that ensnared him. "You should have told me."

And just how was she supposed to have

worked *that* into the conversation? "I didn't think of putting it into my letterhead. Sorry."

Collin caressed her cheek. "No, I'm the one who's sorry."

Something tightened within her, braced for a verbal blow to her pride. "Why, because it wasn't exciting enough for you?"

He could only stare at her, dumfounded. "Where the hell did you get that idea?"

Because it was only logical. But she made no more guesses. "Then why are you sorry?"

"Because, if I'd known, I would have gone slower." There was no point in saying that he wouldn't have touched her. That would have meant he was a saint, of the plaster variety, and they both knew that wasn't true. "I would've made it better for you."

She couldn't see how. Her world was still spinning minutes after the act. "Now, granted, I have no experience in this area to fall back on, but I don't really think that's possible."

He smiled at her. She was so naive, so sweet in her innocence. He felt a tugging on the heart he could have sworn he'd left in his other suit of clothes. "It's possible."

Slowly the smile budded on her lips, infiltrating her eyes. She nestled in against him. "All right, then, show me."

Warmth had already begun to spread from the point of contact, emanating out to his extremities. Heating up everything in between with antsy anticipation.

"Lucy—"

"See?" she announced with a hint of triumph, "I knew it wasn't possible."

He laughed, gathering her back into his arms, pulling her against him like a tight package. He was wanting her all over again.

That, he realized, had never happened before. When he'd made love, it was once and done, the chemistry was gone, like elements drained out of a test tube. But now someone was mysteriously, magically, refilling the test tube and all systems were go again.

"Oh," Collin assured her, "it's possible, all right."

Lucy wiggled against him provocatively, trying out feminine wiles she had never tested before. It was a heady experience.

"Put your money where your mouth is, Military Man."

Collin turned toward the living room where his pants had been tossed, and with them, his wallet, and asked in a deadpan voice, "You want money?"

She framed his face with her hands, bringing it back so that she could look up at him. "You know, for a quiet man, you talk an awful lot."

The next moment she was bringing his mouth down on hers.

And all conversation stopped.

Chapter 13

Lucy knew that she'd never felt like this before. As if she jumped up, she could just about graze the sky with her outstretched fingertips. She felt as if there were no limitations and everything, *everything,* was a possibility.

And it was all because of Collin.

The next time she'd faced him, after their initial night of lovemaking, she'd been nervous. Afraid that Collin would act indifferent toward her, as if all that passion, that wondrous lovemaking she'd experienced for the very first time, had never happened. Afraid that it meant nothing to him.

But there was a warmth to Collin that there

hadn't been before. And when he looked at her, when their hands accidentally touched in passing as they both reached for the papers she'd dropped, there was an intimacy there.

They made love again the next day.

And the day after that and the day after that.

Though she still worked hard at the medical examiner's office, Lucy found herself counting the hours, the minutes, the seconds until she could see him again. She was still trying to help him, still trying to put all the pieces together so that he could locate Jason. But that wasn't her main focus.

Heaven help her, her attention was largely on making love with him. The when and the how.

It made her feel as if she had a precious secret that only she and he were privy to. Making love with him made her feel as if she were glowing inside. So much so that she'd even checked herself over in a mirror once or twice, to see if there was some kind of aura shining around her to give her secret away. Each time she looked and saw nothing but her beaming smile, she wondered how that much radiance could be locked away inside.

Her day no longer began at seven in the morning. It began when she finished her work at the M.E.'s office and Collin came by to pick her up. It began when she joined him in *his* work. Not very independent of her, but then, she wasn't really worried about her independence. If she was worried at all, it was about her heart. Because she knew that no matter what she'd said to the contrary, her heart was no longer in her possession. It was in his.

Picket fences.

She made Collin think of picket fences. The kind that surrounded an idyllic house that had a dog and two point five children playing in the front yard. He wasn't even sure just when it happened, it just had.

The nature of his work kept him on the move. It was the way he'd always liked it. But for the first time in his life, part of him was beginning to wonder what it would feel like to settle down in one place. With one woman.

The woman.

And, for the first time in Collin's life, thoughts about a woman were seeping into his mind completely unbidden. Lucy would just pop into his head while he was talking to Emmett, or still trying to ascertain just where Jason had gotten himself to. After finding traces of his fugitive cousin in the cave, it appeared as if Jason Jamison had somehow managed to disappear off the face of the earth.

Maybe his cousin had gotten smart and had left the area, the county. Maybe even the country. Everything seemed to point in that direction. Except that he knew Jason, knew the way a mind like that, obsessed with the destruction of one man, thought.

Jason, he felt, still had to be here somewhere. But where?

Finding Jason should have been his chief concern, but it wasn't. His chief concern, like it or not, was what he was going to do about feeling this way about Lucy. Did he act on it? Did he just enjoy it and let nature take its course, whatever that turned out to be? The last time he'd sat back and allowed that to happen, albeit unconsciously, the woman in his life had disappeared out of it.

But, looking back, he realized that he hadn't felt about Paula the way he did now about Lucy. Visions of Paula never intruded into his thoughts the way visions of Lucy did. She hadn't commandeered his every thought, hijacking it away from the things he should have been doing.

She hadn't stolen his breath away every time

he thought of her, the way Lucy did whenever he thought of her.

"A penny for your thoughts," Lucy murmured. She tucked her bare feet under her on the sofa and curled into him.

They were at her place again, where they'd seemed to wind up every night for the past week. It was a ritual she knew she could easily become accustomed to. A ritual she already started looking forward to the moment he walked away from her apartment in the morning.

Miss you already, her mind would whisper to his departing back, although she hadn't the courage to let the words find their way to her lips. Not yet. She knew that would only manage to frighten him away.

Heaven knew, it frightened her sometimes to feel this way.

Collin thought of the hopeless battle in which his thoughts were deadlocked. "It'll take a lot more than a penny to ransom them," he told her.

What an odd word to use, she thought. Ransom. As if they were being held prisoner. She wondered if he had a clue that she felt as if all of her had been taken prisoner by him. And that she was more than cheerfully willing to do her time.

She grinned at him. "That's okay. I've got a bank account. I'll write you a check."

Just her smile seemed to open up airless, stuffy rooms within him. Chasing in sunshine and allowing a feeling to come rushing in that he wasn't ready to examine just yet.

Collin pulled her to him, settling her onto his lap. She assumed her new position without protest, her eyes shining as she looked at him.

"And how do I know it won't bounce?" he asked, his face completely sober.

Lucy slipped her arms around his neck. "I guess you'll just have to trust me."

"Trust you," he echoed.

There was still a smile on his face, but a solemnity had slipped into his eyes that she found a little troubling.

Did he trust her?

She knew that, despite all the warnings she'd issued to herself, despite her principles and vows and everything that had come before their first time together, she trusted Collin. Maybe she was being foolish, but there it was. She trusted him.

She'd given him her virginity and her soul all in that same act. And now she trusted him not to break her heart. She refused to believe that he was capable of something like that. She'd waited so long to love a man, really love a man, she wasn't going to ruin it by inflicting doubt into her situation.

"Why?" she teased, bringing her mouth an inch away from his. "Don't you think I'm trustworthy?"

Her breath tantalized him as he felt it along his lips. His gut tightened in anticipation of making love with her.

"Yes," he said, "you are. It's me you should worry about."

She didn't like him saying that. It was as if he was beginning to prepare her for something. For a break. She didn't want him to pledge his undying love or to even make promises about tomorrow. But she didn't want him marring today with seedlings of doubts that promised to grow like weeds.

She looked at him and quietly asked, "Why?"

It was far too complicated for Collin to sum up in a sentence or two. Her life was just beginning. His, on the other hand, was filled with deeds he could never talk about, deeds that had aged him. He'd seen more of life—and death—than she could ever hope to.

"I'm not who you think I am," he told her simply.

Her stomach quivered in fear. But she'd learned to mask her thoughts nearly as well as he did. "Do you have a secret identity, too?"

His eyes narrowed as he looked at her. "Too?"

"Like my mother," she explained.

Lucy doubted if she would ever fully get over that, that her mother had led lives she would never know anything about. That the woman who'd laughed and read her endless stories when she was a child lived a life fully apart from her husband and daughter.

She saw the wariness enter his eyes. "Don't worry, I'm not covertly lifting your finger-prints off a wineglass and running it against some database of master criminals or super spies. I know who you are." That really brought out a concerned expression from him, she noted. It worsened when she went on to say, "The man I made love with. That's enough for me."

God, Collin thought, if she only knew the kind of burden she placed on his shoulders with her trust. He wanted to live up to it. To be the man who made promises to her and gave her if not happily-ever-after, the closest thing to it that was humanly possible.

But leopards didn't change their spots and he wasn't sure if he could be anything other than what he was. And what he was wasn't the kind of man she needed in her life. Not on a permanent basis.

She touched his face gently. "Don't look so pensive." The whispered words floated along his skin. The next moment, Lucy was taking the initiative and kissing him.

Heating his blood.

All logical thought came to an abrupt and sudden halt, the way it did every time they came together like this.

The way it did every time her light perfume filled his head, the scent of her body charged his blood.

Collin closed his arms around this woman who'd made such a difference to him in such a short amount of time. He held her against him as the kiss deepened, taking them both hostage.

Willingly hostage.

The next moment he'd bent her so that Lucy found her back against the sofa and he was over her, their bodies sealed in a pact.

By now Collin felt that he was more familiar

with her body than he was with his own. His own was just there to take him from one place to another, hers was for exploring, for relishing, for filling his dreams, which was where she resided with a regularity he found both enticing and scary as hell at the same time.

This was all new to him.

He'd committed himself to his country, to causes, to the Rangers. But when it came to committing himself to a single human being, to this woman, well, that carried ramifications that made him feel unsure of himself and of his decision.

But that was for contemplating when he was free to think. Not now.

Now he just wanted to touch her again, to feel that surge that came from making love with her. From having her naked flesh rub against his, warm, pliant, supple.

And his.

That he was her first still humbled him. Still placed a huge responsibility on him that he wasn't certain he could live up to. He still had to convince himself that, in the long run, he was the best thing for her. And that this wild insanity that occurred each time they came together like this would last. That wanting her like this wasn't completely interfering with his ability to make good judgment calls.

Eager to have her, he peeled back her clothing swiftly, even as he kissed her over and over again. He loved the way Lucy lifted her arms for him to slip the sweater from her body, the way she shifted so that her jeans would slide down her long, supple legs. It was as if she were doing a seductive dance just for him. A modern, abbreviated version of the dance of the seven veils.

Except that he had a hand in it. A hand that skimmed along her body, glorying in the softness, the smoothness, he found there.

"No fair," she breathed when everything that she'd worn that day was in a heap on the floor. "You're still dressed."

Even as the words came from her lips, she was doing her level best to change the situation. To pull his clothes away from him and revel in his hard, taut, nude body. From what she'd seen, Collin had the body not just of a soldier at the prime of his life, but of a Greek god. His arms and chest had muscles and ridges that gave her a thrill just to run her fingertips over them.

And each time she passed her hands over him, caressing him, she succeeded in arousing

them both a little more. She could see, despite
the iron control he exercised over himself, that
she could easily get to him. *Had* gotten to him.
The sense of power and excitement this created within her was something she knew she
would never be able to put into words.

But then, she didn't have to. All she had to
do was to act on it.

And she did.

Their bodies, naked and wanting, tangled.
She raised her hips so that she could absorb
more of him against her. So that she could husband every sensation that was still a whispered
promise of things to come. He'd already taken
her to regions she hadn't, even in her wildest
imagination, known could exist. He'd already
caused explosions to rack her body in the most
delicious of fashions.

Making love with him was like booking a
tour to a wonderful fantasyland. Lucy discovered that she could react to him on a hundred
different levels. That she was sensitive in so
many different places along her flesh. When
he kissed the right side of her neck, the inside
of her elbow, the area behind her knees, explosions would occur within her.

When he would run his tongue along her
quivering belly, trailing down to the very

damp, wanting core of her, Lucy finally understood what the term sweet agony truly meant.

Climax after climax would flow through her, even as she gasped his name, even as she struggled to hold on to reality and somehow turn the tables on him.

She'd never known it could be like this. And it only got better each time they came together.

But even though she loved what he did to her, how she felt when he made love to every part of her, she didn't want to be only the recipient, she wanted to do something to make him want her as much as she wanted him.

But it was hard to act when exhaustion threatened to claim her, when the desire to experience the mini-explosions his mouth and tongue created within her all but overpowered her. The closest she came was to stroking him in all the different ways that seemed to come instinctively to her. Instincts that she'd been heretofore unaware of. Instincts that came to the fore as if he'd silently summoned them into existence.

She enjoyed her role, loved seeing the look on his face, as if she'd reduced him to a mass of palpitating flesh—just as he had done to her. She closed her hand around him, moving her fingers rhythmically. He was hard and wanting against her palm.

But before she could bring him up to the final moment, Collin placed his hand over hers, stilling all movement. As she looked at him quizzically, he pressed her back against the sofa again and raised himself over her.

"Was I doing it wrong?" she asked.

The laugh was unexpected. "No, you were doing it just right. That's the trouble."

She didn't understand.

But there was no time to ask him to explain. The next moment he was sheathing himself within her, moving the very earth beneath her.

The dance began, the tempo taking her to another place, another realm. Somewhere far away. She raced to keep up, her breath growing shorter and shorter as the marathon took them both up to the very highest peak imaginable and left them tottering there as the fireworks exploded all around them.

Lucy dug her fingertips into his back as the explosion encased her in waves of sensations.

She couldn't ever remember being happier.

The melody was faint.

A call to arms was echoing somewhere distantly from his realm of consciousness.

And then, as he struggled against the effects of a sex-induced sleep, Collin woke up.

The second he did, he realized it was his cell phone that was disturbing the air around him. The cell phone he'd left on her nightstand between the times that they had made love tonight.

He glanced over toward Lucy. She was asleep and curled up against him. The room had a slight chill to it, but the sheet was bunched up and to the side, allowing him to look at her. She lay there, naked and just about the most beautiful sight he had ever seen.

The only thing that rivaled it, that rivaled the feeling inside of him right at this moment, was when he'd looked out of his plane and had seen the approaching coastline of the United States up ahead of him after an eighteen-month assignment in the Middle East.

The word *home* had echoed through his mind at the time.

It was, he realized, the way he viewed her now.

Home.

Easing his body away from Lucy so that he wouldn't disturb her, he picked up the phone and flipped it open. "Jamison," he whispered.

"Lieutenant, I'm afraid we're going to have

to cut your vacation short. There's a matter before me that needs your attention. I'd like you to come back to Virginia."

It was Eagleton. The colonel had no need to introduce himself. Collin would have known his C.O.'s voice anywhere.

A resignation came over him. And with it, a melancholy feeling he was utterly unfamiliar with. He'd never faced an assignment feeling like this before. "When, sir?"

He knew the answer even before the C.O. gave it. "As soon as possible."

That meant as soon as he could catch a flight back. Collin dragged his hand over his face, trying to pull himself together.

Damn.

Nothing was resolved on this end, not the reason he'd come here in the first place nor anything that had happened here since.

For the first time in his life Collin found himself questioning his career choice.

But this wasn't the time to voice any objections. "Right away, sir."

"I'll look forward to seeing you."

With that, the other end of the line went dead. Collin let out a long, steady breath as he closed his cell phone.

Behind him, he heard Lucy stirring on the

bed. He debated waking her, telling her he had to leave and why, but then decided against it. It was still very early. He needed to pack, to get ready. There was no reason to wake her yet. He'd come back just before he was set to fly out to Virginia.

He allowed himself one last, long look before leaving the room, his clothes in his arms. Goodbyes were said more easily if one or more of the parties wasn't naked.

Sleep left her in stages. Like a cloud that was slowly slipping away from a blue sky.

She was reluctant to give it up. Last night and this morning were still very fresh in her mind, their imprint still fresh on her body.

She could feel it tingling and she smiled to herself. Maybe, with a little encouragement, she could get Collin to give a repeat performance just before he left to meet Emmett this morning.

Her smile deepened as her body began to throb with anticipation. He'd outdone himself the last time. The crescendo of climaxes had seemed endless. Tracking wasn't the only thing the man excelled in.

Her eyes still closed, Lucy stretched her hand out to reach for Collin.

Only empty space met her fingertips. A frown curved her mouth. Was she still dreaming? She'd dreamed that he'd left her in the middle of the night, taking away all traces of himself. As if he'd never been in her life. She'd gone from room to room, looking for him, growing increasingly more panicky.

And just when she'd come to the conclusion that he'd disappeared, he'd come out of the shadows, caught her up by the waist and made love with her all over again.

But it had taken a long time for her heart to stop pounding.

Her eyes still closed, a little out of fear this time, she reached farther on the bed.

And still found nothing.

Like an army marching over the field of battle, daylight rolled into her brain, bringing with it an awareness she didn't want.

She opened her eyes.

Collin wasn't here. Moreover, his side of the bed was cool. He'd left her side more than just a few moments ago.

Lucy sat up. Fear instantly gripped her heart. She had no way of explaining it, nothing to point to, but she knew. Knew he had left. Not just her bed, or her apartment, but her.

Getting out of bed, Lucy looked around in

vain for a note, for something that would explain his sudden exodus.

But there wasn't any note.

Neither was there any sign of the clothes they had brought into the bedroom as an afterthought. At least, not his.

He was gone.

Taking a deep breath, Lucy told herself to remain calm. That there was no reason, beyond her unfounded fear, to panic this way.

She panicked anyway. She couldn't help it. When she'd been in love with Jeff, the climate within her world had changed just as suddenly. One day everything had been perfect, the next, the walls came crumbling down, sealing her away from him.

It was happening again. Why else hadn't he woken her up to say he was leaving? That he had an appointment he'd forgotten about? That Emmett had called and asked to see him? There was no plausible explanation.

Grabbing her robe, nurturing a hope she knew was groundless but prayed wasn't, Lucy hurried out of the bedroom.

"Collin?" There was no answer. She raised her voice and called again. "Collin?"

Only the sound of her own breathing echoed back to her within the empty apartment.

She was right. He was gone.

Chapter 14

It had to be done.

Disgruntled, Jason threw down the newspaper he had just been scanning and stepped over it to the hotel window. The window looked out onto an alley, allowing only a moderate amount of light. The third-rate accommodations weren't to his liking, but freedom was. No one would think of looking for him here.

Jason blew out a breath as he glanced back at the paper. At his thoughts.

He didn't like having to trust someone else to do what needed to be done, but it was too dangerous for him to show his face in as public a place as the hospital. Disguised or not, someone might recognize him, especially the closer he got to the guard's ICU. There was a limit to how charmed his life was.

Jason clenched his fists at his sides in a fit of impotence.

Why couldn't that bastard just die instead of lingering like this? Each day Jason scanned the paper, listened to the news, but there was no indication that the second guard had done what he'd been supposed to do and died.

He couldn't wait any longer. The transport guard had to be eliminated. And Jason was going to have to trust someone. For at least a little while. Until the deed was executed and the man returned to him to report on his success.

He knew just the man to use.

Putting on a Stetson and a pair of sunglasses, Jason shrugged into his jacket and went outside to find a pay phone.

Collin made up his mind as he packed.

With each piece of clothing he tossed into the mouth of his duffel bag, his resolution became that much firmer. He was going to ask Colonel Eagleton for a reassignment. As far as he was concerned, his globe-trotting, bullet-dodging days were over. He'd put in his time and earned the right to enjoy life at a less hazardous pace.

If Lucy hadn't come along, he would have continued on this path because he'd had nothing else to compare it to. But she *had* come along and now what he had been doing up until this point, while eminently necessary, no longer called to him. He hadn't done it to satisfy some wanderlust, some crying need for living his life on the edge in the first place.

Yes, it had been exciting, and maybe, during some heat-filled summer evening in the future, when the only sounds to be heard were crickets calling to one another, he might grow nostalgic for the life he'd led. But he knew the feeling wouldn't last. The moment he'd slip his arm around Lucy's waist, pulling her to him, the nostalgia for days past would evaporate like a drop of water on the ground during a heat wave.

Funny how life arranged itself. He now felt that his place was here, with her.

Opening the medicine cabinet, he took out his shaving equipment and placed it inside a small black, zippered pouch before that, too, went into the duffel bag.

He didn't have it all figured out yet, but that would come in time. The first step was to be in the same general area as the woman of his dreams. Because that was what she was. The woman of his dreams—and he hadn't even known he was dreaming of her, until she'd become a reality.

Collin glanced to see that his reflection in the mirror over the small bureau was smiling at him. It wasn't an expression that his face at rest was accustomed to assuming. But loving Lucy made him feel like smiling.

There, he'd admitted it to himself. *I love Lucy.* Who would have ever thought that the title of a sitcom would also define the best part of his life?

His grin grew wider.

He was psyched to put in for his transfer the moment he walked into Eagleton's office. Undoubtedly it would take time to arrange, nothing ever moved fast in the military except for the bullets, but he was determined to get the gears in motion. The last time he'd sat back where his private life was concerned, he'd lost the woman he loved. For some unknown reason he'd gotten lucky and found someone he cared about even more. Lightning didn't often strike in the same place twice. This time he wasn't taking any chances.

Collin took the last of his clothes out of

the closet and tossed them onto the bed. He took the shirts, two at a time, folded them and shoved them into his bag. There wasn't much time before his flight and he wanted to stop by Lucy's and say goodbye. The knock on the door stopped his packing. Who was that?

He'd already talked to Emmett this morning about needing to get back to Virginia. His cousin had been on his way out, doggedly determined to follow up on yet another lead and had merely nodded his assent, asking him to give him a call if he could get back.

He had to hand it to Emmett. He'd never encountered such single-minded purpose before, in or out of the military.

Was that him now? Had his cousin forgotten to tell him something?

"Make it fast, Emmett," he said as he began to open the door. "I'm in a hurry."

The words cut through her like the serrated blade Jason had used so ruthlessly in his bid for freedom.

Lucy raised her chin defiantly. "To escape?" she asked.

The sound of his voice, the echo of his words, unleashed a fury inside of her she hadn't realized she was struggling to keep in check. Just looking at him, packing up his gear, was like standing still for a punch to the gut.

She'd been right. Collin was leaving.

Just like that.

How could he? How could Collin just up and leave her like this, without a word? Without even waking her? She'd trusted this man with her heart and he was deserting her.

She'd been so certain she knew him, and yet, here he was, just like any other man. Obviously what had happened between them had been just a casual fling for him, nothing more.

He looked surprised to see her and all he said was "Lucy."

She pulled her shoulders back. Pulled her tears back, as well. "Well, you remember the name. I guess that's something."

Collin stared at her as he shut the door. "Why shouldn't I remember your name?"

She didn't bother answering that. Instead she looked at the duffel bag on his bed. The khaki bag lay there, mocking her. His belongings were spilling out of its mouth.

"You're leaving." It wasn't a question, it was more like a death sentence. To everything she'd so foolishly thought she had.

He glanced at the bag involuntarily, as if it

served to answer her question. "Yes, the colonel called this morning."

And she just bet that Collin couldn't wait to jump on that plane, to get away from her.

Damn you, Collin Jamison. Damn that heart of yours that wouldn't open up to me.

It took effort, but Lucy got herself back under control as she walked over to the bed. Carefully, she refolded the last shirt he'd dropped beside the bag. She wanted to scream at him, to demand to know why he'd slipped away like some thief in the night instead of waking her to tell her he had to go. To tell her that he didn't want to, but he had to. To tell her that maybe, just maybe, he'd be back. She would have forgiven him anything, as long as she felt that he cared.

But he didn't care, did he? The fact that he'd left her without a word proved that.

"Long assignment?" she asked casually, silently congratulating herself for keeping her voice aloof, distant.

"I don't know yet." He wanted to tell her that he'd be back as soon as he could, but he didn't want to give her any false hopes as to when that would be if he couldn't get his transfer. The colonel might not let him put in for a transfer unless he'd finished whatever it was that he'd been assigned. "I'll call you when I find out," he tagged on almost as an afterthought.

Don't do me any little favors. Lucy shrugged carelessly. "Whatever." She tucked in the last shirt on top of the others, then stepped back from the bed. *That's that, isn't it?* She struggled not to let her voice crack. "Well, godspeed, or whatever it is they say in this kind of a situation." She pretended to look at her watch but in reality saw nothing except her own heartbreak looming in front of her. "I'd better be getting on to the M.E.'s office."

Collin didn't like her tone. It was strained, cool. As if they were strangers who had only now met. As if she'd just happened to pass by his hotel room, with its door ajar, and paused to look in.

He shifted in front of her as she began to leave. "Are you angry about something?"

Yes, you jerk. I'm angry because I fell for you. I'm angry because now that you got more than just a piece of me, you're flying away without so much as a backward glance. Most of all, I'm angry because I don't think I can get over you. Not for a long, long time.

With supreme effort, Lucy pasted a careless smile on her lips. "Not a thing. See you, Military Man." And with that, she walked out.

Had he not been so stunned by her blasé attitude, he would have stopped Lucy and put more questions to her. But because he was stunned, he wasn't reacting like the professional he was, ready for absolutely anything. He was reacting like a man who'd allowed himself to become vulnerable. This was an entirely new role for him.

Hence, speed was not with him. By the time he did react, the door had already closed behind her departing figure.

Coming to, he moved quickly and pulled the door open again.

"Lucy!"

But she was nowhere in sight. He looked up and down the hall. It was as if she'd just evaporated into thin air. As if he'd imagined all of this.

What the hell had just happened here?

He was still wondering that as he boarded his plane half an hour later.

Damn it, if he lived to be a hundred, he wasn't going to understand women. Here he was, ready to turn his whole life inside out and around for her and she was acting as if he was some odious creature that had just crawled out from under a rock. He had half a mind to forget about everything, about her, about his plans for settling down in Texas, and just go on with his life as if nothing had happened.

But something had.

He'd discovered that he had a heart. A heart that could be bruised and...

His own thoughts, usually so organized, echoed back to him in a jumble of half-formed words and sentences, making him feel as if there was something he was missing, some clue he was overlooking.

Lucy really had him going....

And then he realized that here he was, making all these plans for the two of them, and he hadn't told her word one about any of it. He'd left her bed in silence and kept up that silence. She'd surprised him so much, popping up at his hotel room, he hadn't had a chance to say anything to her about it. About coming back to her. About their future.

He thought back to what Emmett had said to him in the restaurant. Wow, he really was lousy at this male-female thing, wasn't he?

The next thought hit him like a thunderbolt. What if Lucy thought that he had intended to leave her without telling her that he was going?

That was it, wasn't it? That was why she'd acted the way she had when she'd come to the hotel room. Because she thought she'd caught him in the act of abandoning her.

Damn it, how could she think that of him?

Well, had he given her any cause not to? He'd left her bed, hadn't he? Without a note, without anything. Never getting a chance to make this right.

Concerned, he took out his cell phone to call her. Punching in the numbers on the keyboard, he listened to the phone ring on the other end.

And ring and ring until finally a tinny voice came on, telling him that the mobile phone party was either out of the area or not answering his cell phone.

"No kidding, Sherlock." Collin didn't bother swallowing the curse that rose to his lips as he shut his phone.

Unbuckling his seat belt, he rose and headed straight for the cockpit.

Lucy felt as if she were sleepwalking. As if she were being held in the grasp of some horrible, unending nightmare.

Her prince had turned out to be a troll.

No, that wasn't right, either, she corrected miserably. Collin hadn't made her any promises. Not verbally, anyway, she thought rebelliously.

But silently, with his eyes, with his touch, there were promises made. Pledges of eternity. Didn't that count?

She shoved the middle drawer shut. Hard enough to send some papers flying off the desk and to the floor. She bent to pick them up.

"Stop it," she lectured herself angrily. "You're twenty-six years old, grow up, for God's sake, Luce."

"Is this a private conversation or can anyone get in?"

Startled, she looked up and saw that Harley was in the doorway, watching her.

Embarrassed, she rose to her feet, even though for the life of her she had no idea where she was going next. She tossed her head before she looked up at him.

"It's a private argument, but it's over." *Really over.* "What do you need?"

The portly man answered without hesitation. "My bank account tripled, chocolate cake to be declared a necessary food supplement and a date for Saturday night. But I came here to tell you something I thought you might be interested in, given your prior supposedly 'covert' activity." He ended the sentence with a broad grin.

She'd come to consider Dr. Harley Daniels a friend and right now she was dying for something to sink her teeth and mind into, something that would take her thoughts off this incredible pain that was shredding her apart bit by bit.

Lucy strove to center all her attention on what he was saying. "Oh?"

"That guard you were so interested in? The one involved in that maniac's prison escape?"

Impatience didn't just weave in and out of her, it was doing a major number on her nerves. She struggled to keep her voice calm. "Yes, what about him?"

Harley took a candy bar out of the deep pockets of his lab coat and began to unwrap it with great care, as if it was bordering on a religious experience. "Word has it that he's regained consciousness. He's been floating in and out for the last few hours."

"How do you know that?"

He winked at her. "We amiable types have our ways." Harley took a bite out of the bar, then added, "The FBI is hopeful that he might be able to give them a coherent statement sometime late today or possibly tomorrow morning."

She didn't even bother to pretend to deny that she was somehow following the case, trying to take an active part. Harley might have had his faults, but one of them wasn't stupidity.

Lucy remembered her promise to Collin, that she'd let him know if she heard anything new about the search for Jason. This might be the break he was looking for. Certainly nothing else had turned up lately.

Her fingers curled around the cell phone in her pocket. She thought of calling Collin with the news, but knew she couldn't hear the sound of his voice without falling apart. Besides, what did she have to tell him? Third-hand information. It would be better if she went to see the guard herself, see what she could ascertain. And, if there was anything to tell, maybe she would contact Collin's cousin Emmett instead. After all, Jason was his brother.

She felt as if all her thoughts were colliding with one another. She wasn't used to feeling this web of confusion closing in tightly around her brain.

"Oh," she said again, trying desperately to reform her thoughts into something coherent.

She needed to see the guard herself. As soon as possible.

Lucy pressed her lips together and looked at Harley. "Could I—?"

Harley was way ahead of her. Tossing the candy bar wrapper into the wastepaper basket, he waved her out of the room. "Go, go. I'll cover for you."

She smiled at him. "Thanks." Lucy started for the door.

"Sure. Anything to get that look off."

She stopped short and turned around. "'Look'?" she echoed.

"Yeah. The one on your face right now." He took a step closer to her as he made the observation, his voice kindly rather than teasing. "You look as if you've just lost your best friend."

"No," she said quietly, looking at him pointedly. "All my friends are exactly where they always were." She'd just made a mistake in counting someone new in their number, she added silently.

Harley went to the locker she never kept locked. Opening the door, he took her jacket off the hook and held it out to her. "I think we need another sample of his DNA. I misplaced the last sample."

She knew he hadn't done any such thing and, as far as the coroner's office was concerned, there was no real need for any sample in the first place. Harley was giving her an excuse to see the guard. He was taking the blame for the visit away from her.

Taking her jacket, Lucy paused to brush a quick kiss to his rounded cheek. "You're the best."

Harley flashed her a grin as he made his way out through the back entrance. "Tell me something I don't already know."

There was a new policeman outside the guard's ICU door. Smaller than the first man, dark in coloring, with an air of preoccupation about him, the officer looked like less of a threat than even the first policeman had been. Reading a manual whose cover she couldn't quite make out, the officer looked up in Lucy's direction as she approached. But because she was wearing her white lab jacket and an ID hanging from a chord around her neck, the glance he afforded her was only cursory.

It was obvious to Lucy that the police were only going through the motions since there'd been no threat to the injured guard's life so far. Apparently everyone was of the same mind, that Jason was far too smart to attempt anything here at the hospital. Most likely, the man charged with two murders was as far away from Red Rock as was humanly possible in the amount of time he had.

Carrying the tray with several innocuous-looking little white paper cups that usually contained medication and that she had purloined from the nurses' station when no one was looking, Lucy flashed a smile at the young policeman and eased herself into the transport guard's room.

Once the door was closed, she released the breath she'd been holding. She put the tray down on the closest surface and approached the bed. There were several fewer machines surrounding him than there had been the last time she'd been in the room.

The transport guard appeared to be asleep. Had he slipped back into a coma? God, she hoped not. Lucy looked at the vital signs for a clue.

Everything appeared to be normal.

Her heart slipped up into her throat as Lucy placed her hand on the man's arm and just barely shook it. "Mr. McGruder?"

In response, his eyelids flew open and she found herself looking into a pair of almost-clear blue eyes that were staring straight at her.

It took her a second to find her tongue. "Mr. McGruder, I'm with the medical examiner's office and I have to ask you some questions."

"Why are you disturbing the patient?" a deep voice growled behind her.

Startled, Lucy swung around toward the door. The somewhat average-looking man was frowning at her as he came forward. The lab coat he had on seemed a size too large for him and it flapped around his legs as he moved.

"You need to leave," he told her curtly. "Now." The word was issued like a royal command.

He probably thought she was a nurse. And he undoubtedly was one of those doctors who believed he walked on water, she judged, and had no use for anyone who couldn't do the same thing. Her immediate response was anger, despite the fact that she actually had no business being here.

It had been that kind of a day.

Looking back, she would never be able to explain why she hadn't merely obeyed and left the room, why the man's tone set something off inside of her, making her not only angry, but more than mildly uneasy.

She thought of her cover story. "I'm from the M.E.'s office," she informed him, lightly running her hand over her hanging ID tag. "I need to get a DNA sample from the patient."

His expression darkened, but he waved her over to the bed grudgingly. "All right, be quick about it."

The hand that had waved at her had dirt under its nails. A quick glance told her that the same was true of the other hand. Alarms went off in her head. No doctor would be seeing patients with hands like that.

Something was wrong here.

Lucy suddenly felt the urgency to stall for time. Striving for her friendliest manner, she put out her hand. "Hi, I'm Lucy Gatling."

He made no effort to take her hand or to offer his own. "And I'm in a hurry. Do what you have to do and leave," he ordered.

She looked at his hands again. "Shouldn't you be washing your hands?"

He glanced at his hands, saw his error and cursed roundly. "The hell with this."

The next moment Lucy found herself staring down the extended barrel of his weapon. There was a silencer on the end of it.

Chapter 15

Collin threw his duffel bag into the back seat of the car he'd rented at the airport and drove to the coroner's office. It probably would have been cheaper in the long run to hail a cab, but he was impatient enough as it was. Sitting in the backseat, leaving the driving to someone else, would have been unbearable.

At this time of day the traffic was only moderately busy. He maneuvered the subcompact in and out of tight spots, jockeying for position, intent on beating all the lights.

So far, so good.

Collin forced himself to relax his grip on the steering wheel. It took conscious effort.

He felt as if every nerve inside his body was standing at attention as he reviewed what he was going to say to Lucy. He'd been calmer facing an armed assailant. The only thing that would have made him more nervous was leaving things the way they were until later.

He'd learned his lesson well. Later would be too late.

Eagleton had been surprised, to say the least, when he'd talked to him. The C.O. had expected to see him in person. Instead, the call had come in from his cell phone after he'd had the plane turn around. He'd made his case as quickly, as succinctly, as possible

Because of his spotless record and his dedication, which went above and beyond the call of duty by anyone's measure, and despite his unorthodox behavior this time around, Collin obtained the leeway he needed.

"A few hours, sir," he'd concluded. "I just need a few more hours before reporting in."

There was a long pause before Eagleton replied. "This is highly unusual, Collin, but then, so are you."

It had taken the colonel five years and a mission behind enemy lines that they weathered together for the informality between them to take hold and grow. And another three years before that for the rapport that they now had to be shared. Collin knew, though the man had only come close to telling him once, when three sniper bullets had sent the colonel to what everyone had thought was his deathbed, that Eagleton regarded him as the son he'd never had.

The feeling was mutual. Collin thought of him as a second, albeit more stern, father.

"I wouldn't ask if it wasn't important," Collin had assured him.

"I know. Which is why I'm granting you the extra time. But no more than a few hours," Eagleton had warned.

A time had been set, the connection terminated. And Collin was off and running the second the plane had landed back at the airport.

A few hours was all Collin felt he needed to make his case with Lucy. To make her agree to see what the future held in store for them. Together.

The open parking lot directly in front of the building that housed the coroner's offices was full. He was forced to leave his rented vehicle within the bowels of the parking structure at the other end of the lot. Collin all but sprinted across the lot and into the building.

Something inside of him felt as if time was slipping through his fingers. He didn't know why. Maybe because now that he'd finally made up his mind on what course he wanted to take, he was eager to begin.

Words tripping over one another in his head, he made his way into the medical examiner's offices, to the area where Lucy generally did her work.

She wasn't there.

A quick search showed him that she wasn't anywhere in the immediate area. An uneasiness began to weave through him. He kept on looking, walking into one of the autopsy rooms.

When he saw the doctor who normally worked with her, he felt just a little heartened. The physician, swaddled in blue livery and in the middle of his work, glanced up at him with the look of a man who didn't like being interrupted.

"She's not here," Harley informed him curtly.

"Well, where is she?" Collin wanted to know.

He moved closer to the table where the autopsy was being conducted. The smell coming from the corpse was horrid.

Had he not been accustomed, in a fashion, to the stench of death, Collin was certain last night's dinner would have made a reappearance in his throat, possibly the floor.

Harley's small brown eyes looked at him over the mask he'd donned to help him filter out the immediate unsettling smell. Collin had the distinct impression that he was being judged and appraised.

He was all set to repeat his demand, more harshly now because he wasn't up to playing whatever games the good doctor wanted to play, when the latter told him, "You just missed her by half an hour." It was obvious that Harley debated telling him any more, weighing the pros and cons. The pros won. "She went to find out more information for you. According to what we hear, that transport guard regained consciousness."

If he had any more to say, there was no one to say it to. Collin was already gone.

With one eye on the rearview mirror, watching for approaching police vehicles, Collin drove to the hospital like a man possessed. All the way there he couldn't really explain why, but he had this uneasy feeling that something was wrong. He told himself that it was probably just that he was nervous over what he wanted to say to Lucy, over the commitment he planned to make, but he couldn't quite talk himself into a state of calm. The hairs were standing up on the back of his neck the way they did whenever he was about to go head-to-head with an enemy.

Collin hurried into the hospital, rushing past the admitting desk and toward the bank of elevators in the rear of the building. His adrenaline refused to stop pumping. Every part of him felt as if it was throbbing to a strange rhythm.

Was this what being in love was like? As if you were preparing to go into battle? If that was the case, he supposed he'd been preparing for this from the first day he'd attended West Point.

Reaching the floor that housed the intensive care unit assigned to McGruder, he hurried to the left corridor. The last time he'd approached the room, the figure of a young police officer, his feet indolently stretched out in front of him as he slouched in his chair, was evident from the moment he turned the corner.

The only thing he saw when he turned the corner was an empty chair.

The hairs on the back of Collin's neck refused to go down.

* * *

Lucy's mouth felt dry.

The last few minutes felt like an eternity. Part of her still wanted to edge her way toward the door, to try to attract the attention of the police officer posted right outside the room. She was torn between that and remaining here to somehow save the man asleep in the bed.

The thought that she needed to figure out a way to save herself whispered on the edges of her mind, but Lucy refused to view that as her focus. If this man carried out his plans to kill the transport guard, she was as good as dead herself. The man in the ill-fitting white lab coat didn't look like the type who would leave witnesses standing around.

She tried to appeal to whatever sense of decency might still reside within the man's thick chest. "Look, whatever Jamison said he's paying you to do this, it's not worth killing someone for."

There was contempt in the man's eyes long before it filtered down to the rest of his face. He sneered at her naïveté. "A couple of extra lives don't mean anything to me."

He wasn't lying. She could see it in his eyes. They were flat, devoid of any connection, any humanity, however vague. There was no glee there, either. The transport guard's would-be murderer didn't seem as if he loved his work. It was just a job to him, nothing better, nothing worse. Some people delivered newspapers for a living, he delivered corpses. It was all one and the same to him.

She had nothing to appeal to.

The tray she'd brought in was still sitting on the side table where she'd left it. Lucy thought of making a grab for it and throwing the tray at the man to deflect his aim. It was the only plan she could come up with on such short notice. The fact that the gunman would probably end up shooting at her first couldn't be factored into her decision.

She wished she knew how fast this man was. Was he a trained operative who had gone rogue? An expert in his field the way Collin undoubtedly was in his? At which point he'd probably drop her first, then kill the transport guard and go strolling out of the room, all in under a minute, all with a minimum of sound.

She could feel it in her gut.

If she cried for help, he'd kill her before anyone could reach her.

Her one chance, the way she saw it, was to keep a dialogue going until something happened, someone came in. The only trouble was, she had no way of knowing how long that would be. And he didn't look like someone with an infinite amount of patience.

"If you leave now, I won't tell anyone I saw you." The laugh she got in response sent a chill down her spine. Desperate, she tried another approach. "When you're done here carrying out his orders, are you going back to Jamison for your money?"

She sincerely doubted that Jamison had given the money to the man up front. At most, he might have advanced half, the rest to follow on completion.

The man on the other end of the gun looked unwilling to reveal anything. At the same time, he appeared intrigued by the fact that she wasn't begging for her life. That she was engaging him in a conversation.

"Let's say I am," he said, leaving the rest of the sentence open.

"He'll kill you, you know," she said simply as her stomach continued experiencing a magnitude 9.0 earthquake. She saw anger in the man's eyes and pushed on, watching his weapon warily. "Jamison doesn't like leaving any loose ends, or loose lips."

He snorted, unimpressed by her reasoning. "A lot of men have tried to kill me."

Her eyes remained steadily on his. "All it'll take is one."

The minutes were ticking away and with it the small amount of patience he laid claim to. "Enough talking, bitch." He raised his arm, pointing his weapon straight at her. "Sorry about this, but you had your chance to leave." Nondescript, able to blend in, maybe he'd initially figured she wouldn't have been able to describe him to anyone. But it had gone beyond that now, she knew. "Your bad luck, being so observant."

Her breath stopped as she saw his finger begin to squeeze the trigger.

Suddenly the door behind him flew open, banging against the wall. Lucy made the most of her opportunity. Lunging for the tray, she sent it flying into the gunman's arm.

A slight "ping" was heard as the bullet went wild.

The next moment Lucy was positive she was hallucinating. She had to be. Why else would she think she saw Collin coming to her rescue?

She barely remembered screaming out his name in both relief and horror.

Collin burst into the room, simultaneously hurling himself to the floor, the epitome of a moving target. Rolling, he bounced back up to his feet within inches of the assailant.

The struggle for the weapon was short-lived. Faced with Collin's intensive training in self-defense and warfare, the assailant was quite clearly out of his league. Collin had him disarmed, disabled and on the ground within seconds, his knee pressed hard against the man's square neck as he held the gunman's arm twisted in the air. The latter was gasping for breath even as he was screaming in pain.

The only thing Collin was concerned about was Lucy. He looked at her now as he continued to twist the man's arm up and to the side. "Are you all right?"

She had to take a deep breath before answering. "Fine now that the cavalry's here," she managed to get out. It was next to impossible to talk with her heart pounding in her throat.

Collin looked around the austere room. "I need something to tie him up with." The police were on their way, summoned by his 9-1-1 call, but he was taking no chances.

Lucy hurried to the overhead cabinets, throwing open the doors as she searched for something for him to use. All she came up with was a roll of bandages. She held it up for him to see. "This is all there is."

He held his hand out. "That'll do fine. I don't need much," he assured her. He knew how to truss a prisoner up using nothing more than dental floss if need be.

Lucy handed him the bandages, then watched as he all but gift-wrapped the man on the floor. It was only then that logic slowly returned to her.

"What are you doing here?" She wanted to know. "I thought you were on your way to Virginia."

"I was." Finishing, he tied off the bandage and tested the strength of his work. It would hold, he decided. "And then I realized that all my conversations were in my head."

Confused, Lucy stared at him. She wasn't following Collin. "What conversations?"

"Conversations I'd had about the future." He looked at her as he slowly got off the prisoner and watched the man for any false moves. The assailant lay there as if all the air had been siphoned out of him. Collin slanted her a look. "Our future."

She had to have slipped into shock. Why else was she hearing what she so desperately wanted to hear? There was this buzzing in her head that conflicted with coherent thought. Still, she heard herself asking, "We have a future?"

He looked at her meaningfully. "We do if you want us to."

Oh, no, he wasn't going to put this on her shoulders. Her decision, her fault. She wasn't about to let that happen. "Do you want us to?"

He grinned at her. *Nicely done*, he thought. "I'm asking the questions here."

But she shook her head, forgetting all about the man in the bed, the man on the floor. It was just the two of them. Forever loomed just beyond, an enticing prize.

"Sorry, it's not a one-way street." Her pragmatic nature took hold. She was still her mother's daughter. "How's this going to work with you in Virginia and me here?"

"Everything'll work out as long as you want it to." And then, although he hadn't put his request to Eagleton, hadn't begun to wade through the tonnage of paperwork, he told her what was on his mind. She deserved to know. "Besides, I forgot to tell you. I'm putting in for a transfer."

"A transfer?" Her eyes widened as she repeated the words. "To where?"

"Austin." It was close enough to where she

was. A hell of a lot closer than Virginia. Or the Middle East. "As a trainer."

Hospital security men entered the room, interrupting them. Collin backed away from his prisoner, placing a protective arm around Lucy. "The police are on their way," he told them. "There's an officer in the supply closet you might want someone to see to." The would-be assassin had apparently dragged the unsuspecting officer there after knocking him out. That was where he'd found the man. "He's got a nasty gash on his forehead."

His arm around Lucy's shoulders, he pulled her to the side, away from the security people and closer to him. "Now, before this really gets crazy here, where was I?"

"Transferring. And becoming a trainer." It all sounded too good to be true. And she'd learned a long time ago that if something seemed too good to be true, it usually was. Still, she mentally crossed her fingers as she looked up at Collin. "You can really do this?"

"It'll take some time," he warned her. "The paperwork has to go in and the wheels within any government agency turn slowly." Then he grinned. "But yeah, I think it can be done."

Her eyes remained on his, looking for answers, for something she could expand on. "Do you *want* to do this?" she pressed.

He laughed. This was why he loved her. Because she could look into his heart and see things about him others couldn't. Because she seemed to know him better than he knew himself.

Except that this time she'd misread the signs.

His arm around her tightened. He lowered his voice, bringing his mouth closer to her ear as the commotion behind them grew. "I think maybe it's time I stop trying to save the world and save a little piece of it for myself. Let the younger guys play Bruce Willis."

She frowned a little at his statement. She didn't want him retiring from the world. She wanted him safe, but not at the cost of who he was. "You're not exactly old."

"No." He brushed a lock of her hair from her face, toying with it. "But I've got a reason to go on living now. I didn't before. Having a reason slows you down. Makes you hesitate."

She could swear she felt her heart leap up inside of her. "And what's that reason?"

He smiled down into her eyes, wondering how he thought he was alive before he'd met her. "Can't you tell?"

"Nope, sorry." She shook her head. "I need it spelled out for me."

"Okay. L-o-v-e." Humor played along the corners of his mouth. "That satisfy your spelling needs?"

Love. He loved her. She struggled to contain herself. "Depends," she deadpanned.

He cocked his head, unsure what she was driving at. "On?"

Joy was squeezing out to every corner of her being. It was rough keeping it from her face for even a moment longer as she played out the charade. "On whom that l-o-v-e is aimed at."

His voice softened to a rough whisper. "You. Only you."

Her breath grew short, her pulse intensified. "You really love me?"

"I turned an army transport around for you. Put my C.O. on hold for you. If that's not love, lady, then I don't know what is." He pulled her closer to him, fitting her neatly against his body. "Now, the question before the house is, do you love me?"

With all her heart and soul, she thought. "If you have to ask, Collin, then you're not as smart as I thought you were."

Too many things in his world went unspoken. This, he needed to hear. "I'm just a simple soldier at heart. But even simple soldiers need love."

"You have love, Military Man." Lucy moved her body even closer against his, fusing their energy. "You had it almost right from the start."

"Start," he echoed with a smile, nodding his head in approval. "I like the sound of that word. Means the beginning of a brand-new adventure."

"You're going to be having all your adventures at home with me," she informed him.

"Hey," he said just as the room began to fill up with policemen and more security personnel, "sounds good to me. You're all the adventure I'll ever need."

Her eyes were dancing as she laced her arms around his neck. "You got that right."

He began to kiss her, then stopped. He wanted to make sure everything was perfectly clear. He had a habit of taking things as a given. Which meant taking them for granted. He didn't want that to happen with her. Ever. "You do understand that I'm asking you to marry me, right?"

It took her a second to recover. That was something she most definitely *hadn't* understood from the conversation. Everything inside of her shouted with joy.

"Good thing you're good with your hands, Military Man, because your verbal skills..." Lucy held her hand out and waffled it back and forth in the air. "Not so much." Lacing her hand around his neck, she grinned up at him. "But we'll work on it."

"The answer, woman. What's the answer?"

Her eyes danced. "What do you think the answer is?"

"I think yes."

Ignoring the other people in the room for a moment longer, she stood up on her toes, her body fitting snugly against his. "Then you get the prize."

"Yeah, I know."

Someone was calling to him, asking questions. He knew he'd have to get back to them by and by, but right now he had something more pressing to attend to. The rest of his life was calling to him. He answered the call with a long, soulful kiss.

* * * * *